# HONESTY
# & 
# LIES

Also by Eloise for Firefly:
Elen's Island
Gaslight
Seaglass
Wilde

# HONESTY & LIES

## ELOISE WILLIAMS

First published in 2022
by Firefly Press
25 Gabalfa Road, Llandaff North, Cardiff, CF14 2JJ
www.fireflypress.co.uk

Text copyright © Eloise Williams 2022

The author asserts her moral right to be identified as author in accordance with the Copyright, Designs and Patent Act, 1988.

All rights reserved.
This book is sold subject to the condition that it shall not, by way of trade or otherwise, be lent, resold, hired out or otherwise circulated without the publisher's prior consent in any form, binding or cover other than that in which it is published and without a similar condition including this condition being imposed on the subsequent purchaser.

All characters in this publication are fictitious and any resemblance to real persons, living or dead, is purely coincidental.

A CIP catalogue record of this book is available from the British Library.

1 3 5 7 9 8 6 4 2

Print ISBN 9781913102999
ebook ISBN 9781915444004

*This book has been published with the support of the Books Council of Wales.*

Map illustration by Guy Manning
Chapter heading art by Becka Moor

Printed and bound by CPI Group UK

'Ye eventes showne in this booke are but a fiction.'

For Janine Barnett-Phillips,
Jennifer Killick and Rhian Tracey.
True friends in tough times.

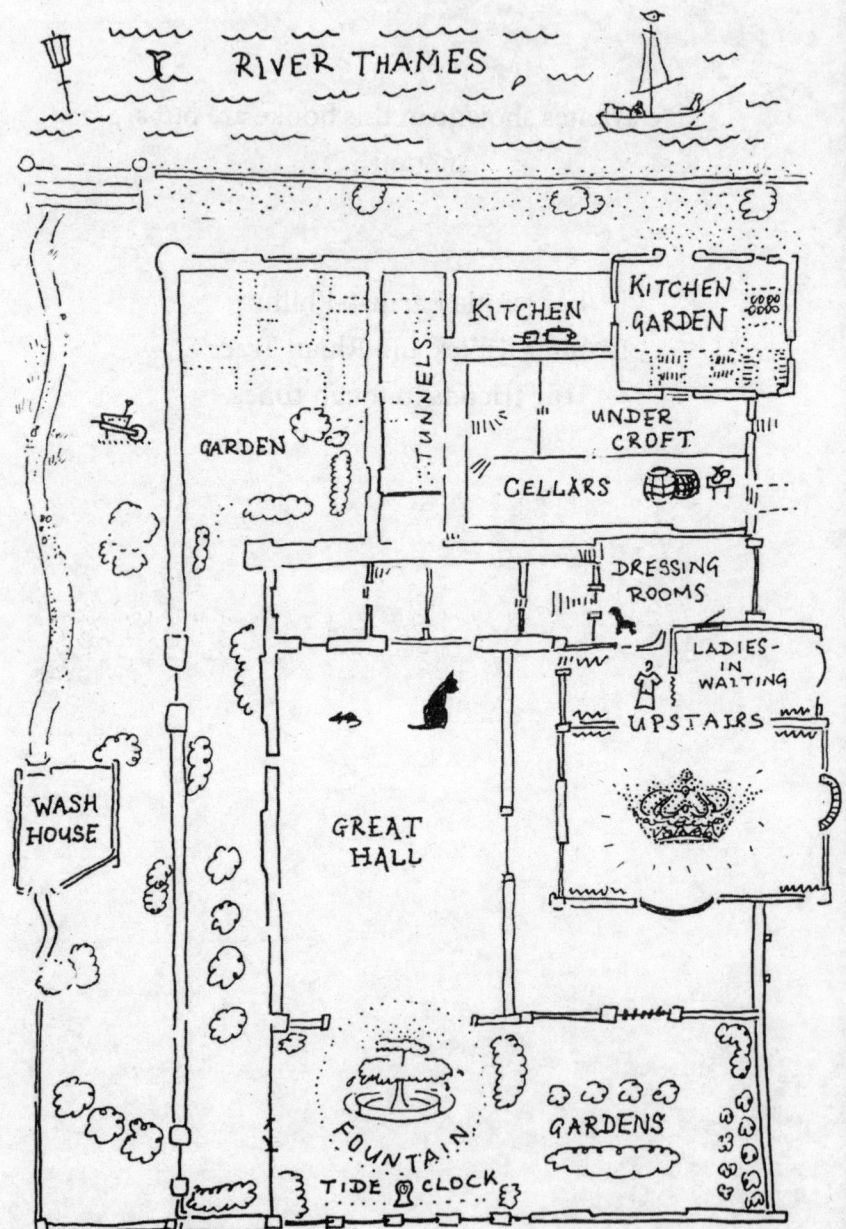

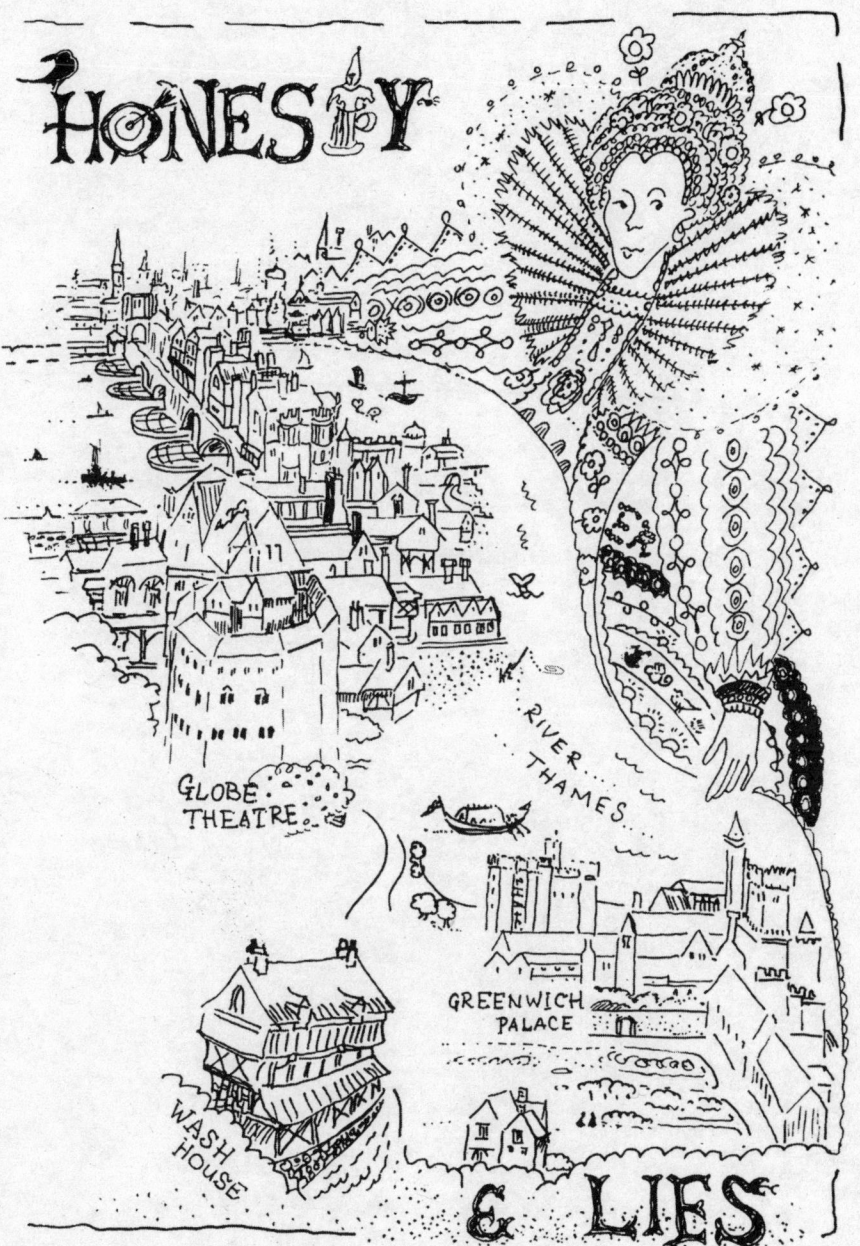

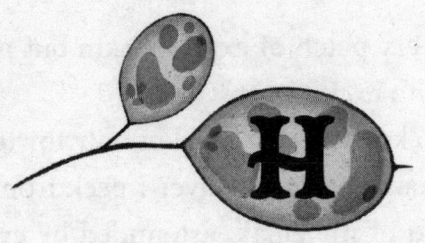

CHAPTER ONE

# HONESTY

'The City of London,' someone shouts as the cart hits a pothole and almost spills me out. I have made it. Never have I seen so many people and never have I smelled so many either. It stinks to high heaven. Bodies and filth and the deep, green stench of the river. The air snaps with cold and icicles hang from every timber and roof.

I climb out as nimbly as I can, having been squashed among cabbages for so long, and thank the farmer, paying him for his kindness. I am wobbling like a newborn foal.

*London.* People everywhere, unloading cargo from vast, weather-beaten ships. Languages I have never heard before bloom into the air. The cold hurts every patch of exposed skin but my cheeks flame with excitement. *London.*

Who knew that I, a girl of only thirteen years, could make it this far alive? I peek from beneath the hood of my cloak, astounded by everything. Two men with hounds drive a flock of sheep to market. Another runs past, carrying a puppet, chased by a string of gabbling children. The bright colours spinning around me are dizzying and wonderful.

It should be easy to blend in here, with people of so many shapes and sizes, but I am still afraid. How terrible it would be for someone to grab me now and force me to return after such a journey. Surely, I am safe here, so far from Wales? But some of the ships look like the ones we get at home in Dinbych-y-Pysgod and I believe in bad luck. I can picture my father sailing up the Thames, appearing here in front of me, shouting and reaching out to catch me in a net, haul me in, and take me back to be whipped. I need to keep moving.

I sidestep some poor seasick soul who is puking over his toes and someone else's heels, and accidentally jolt a sausage seller who shoves me away. My stomach roars. The last meal I had was a blackbird two days ago and a gnaw on a raw cabbage in the cart.

I can see now that all my ideas of what I would find in London are laughable. What opportunities will there be here for a girl with little skill, except for a quick tongue and a way with stories? I cannot tell anyone about my parentage or past. I shall have to rely on my wits. I must make a plan. If I stand still near the riverbank for much longer, my blood will freeze in this ice-flecked air. If I keep moving, perhaps fate will take a chance on me and help me to find hope. I pray it will.

I weave through the crowd, my head bowed against the brunt of the wind. My feet are bloodied and blistered, my hands scratched and covered with filth, but I am here. I am here! I am terrified.

Dodging a rolling barrel, I tack my way between women bartering for cheaper prices, scowling theatrically when they are refused. Just like the women I see every day in the marketplace. Thinking of home, I have to stop, leaning against an overturned boat, my chest heaving with panic. On a warm day it might be exciting to tarry here, watching the world go by, but today I spout white breath like a dragon.

I am a dragon, I tell myself. Brave and proud and

fierce, with fire in my belly. I have made it all the way here and I am not yet dead. I must seek out lodgings before night and soon after find work. The pitifully few coins in my purse will not last me long. I will not despair.

Dread tingles my fingers, and my breath comes in short, sharp bursts. I rub my hands together to stop the fizzing pain. Standing here is not helping me at all. I must be brave and move again.

Christmastide celebrations are well underway, and a group of revellers sing enthusiastically until one of them falls in the river and has to be fished out. Everyone is in festive mood and I'm about to head towards a milling throng to see what fun is drawing them together, when I am grabbed by the wrist.

'Come with me on an adventure,' a gnarled old woman coaxes.

I cannot break away.

Her gums hold no teeth; her eyes are milky yellow; her nails the talons of a hawk. She drags me towards an alley with surprising strength for someone so withered. That is how I know that she is bad. I can taste it like blood on my tongue. Danger. I struggle to get free, a rabbit in a snare. Someone is waiting in the shadows for us, and pure terror makes me strong.

'Let me loose!' Gritting my teeth, I pull back, lift one foot and kick. She collapses and I leave her there in the filth as I run.

You must not trust anyone these days. Everyone knows that London is full of thieves and filchers, rogues and muggers. Worse still, that woman may be a witch. A shudder runs the length of my spine and I hunch my shoulders. Even here, amongst all these people, a witch could kill me with a curse. I speed up. Head down. Getting as far away from her as possible.

'Argh!'

The girl I've bumped into is red-faced with anger. I'm covered in cabbage and dirt and have left a mark on the package she carries.

'I'm so sorry.' Despite my fright, I remember to speak in English. Raising my hands in surrender, I see they are shamefully unclean so knot them behind my back.

'You must learn to look where you are going.' Her voice, though small, is colder than this winter's day. 'This is an item of great importance.'

'There was someone chasing me,' I say in agitation.

Will this girl help me? We are about the same age. From her clothes I can tell she is a person of some means.

'Who?' She eyes me suspiciously. 'Have you done something wrong?'

'No. The woman meant *me* harm. She's gone now.'

She scans the space behind me for pursuers.

I must befriend this girl. Flattery works well at home. 'I know nothing about London at all. I imagine you know many things.'

'I do.' A flicker of thrill crosses her face, which she quickly hides.

I try to appear innocent, but it just makes her examine me more closely. 'If only I knew as much as you,' I add and regret it immediately because she scoffs in reply.

She inspects me, cocking her head this way and that like a chicken. I whimper a little, truly self-pitying, then try a different ruse.

'I need someone knowledgeable who can find me safe lodgings for the night.' Crossing my fingers behind me, I implore her with my eyes. *Please help me. Please.*

Her face shows nothing. I cannot read her thoughts.

Something tells me that I should be sincere

with this girl, but the truth is too frightening, so I make up a story.

'The truth is, I was on a ship as a lady's maid. Unfortunately, a gigantic wave knocked me overboard. I managed to swim to the bank but the ship and all my possessions and everyone I know are now sailing off to...' I search in my mind for foreign places. 'To far-off countries. I don't know what to do.'

This last bit is true at least.

'Your clothes are dry,' Mistress Disdain says. Her scornful manner would make a less dragonhearted girl give in.

'They have dried in this keen wind.'

'A likely story.' She begins to walk away.

'For pity. Please. Please help me.' Something in my wavering voice makes her return.

'You enjoy telling tales, that much I know. You are also up to no good, that much I also know.' She raises a finger to warn me against interrupting. 'Tell me, girl, why should I help you? If we are to get to the truth eventually, we may as well visit it now.'

'If you do not help me, I will surely die.' I feel my lip quiver and clench my hands into fists.

'You have almost ruined my package.' The girl

primly brushes tiny bits of me from her parcel. Even when every last trace of me is completely gone, she keeps fussing. She will wear a hole in the paper if she's not careful.

'What is inside it?' I cannot stem my curiosity. I always want to know about everything. Father says it is a fault I've had since I was born. I put him to the back of my mind and smile encouragingly at the girl. The wrapping is fine quality and sealed with a violet ribbon.

She glances around and leans in whispering, 'Glorious materials for Queen Elizabeth herself.'

I try not to smirk. This girl is either a liar or mad, or as much of a storyteller as me. As if she would be carrying something for the Queen! Turning my smile into a look of wonder, I play along, asking in awe, 'For the Queen herself? I can hardly believe it. What an honour it must be.'

'An honour indeed.' She narrows her eyes, green as early apples and twice as sharp. Now I have her herring-hooked and wriggling, I keep her on the line.

'Tell me, please, how you came to have it in your possession?' This girl has money or good employment and is clean and well fed. I am determined to forge a friendship with her.

'Your voice is peculiar.' Her expression is so scornful, she looks as if she has licked vinegar from a wound. 'It almost sings.'

I laugh and clap my hands together. They ring with the cold and my bones hurt, but it is joyous to think of my voice like this. 'Yes, because I am Welsh.'

'That explains it,' she says, not unkindly but not respectfully either. 'I have an errand to run. I will point you to where you can find rooms for the night. Be quick. I am needed elsewhere.'

I say, 'Thank you,' in English, of course, but only once and curtly. Then I rush after her as she scurries along. Her hair is flaxen-yellow and tendrils of it break free from her hat, tangling back towards me in golden snakes. She is taller than me, her stride is long, and I have to trot to keep up. At least hurrying warms my blood.

I keep an arm's length from her. She seems bright and trustworthy, but villains come in all guises.

As she rushes ahead, I wonder what the planets have written for me and how fortune will treat me now that I am alone. Fate has brought me to this girl, and I must use the cards it has dealt me and all of my energy to keep myself alive.

## CHAPTER TWO
# ALICE

This Welsh girl is short and slow. Turning to check that she is behind me has become like a game of tag. I have no time for games.

'Keep up,' I scold her. She is small and bedraggled; her feet have to take two steps to every one of mine. I try to slow my pace, but the winter bites at my knuckles and dawdling is for lazy days.

Glancing back, I can see that she is amazed by everything around her. Well she might be! Amused by her expression, I view this part of London through a newcomer's eyes. This girl must come from the countryside, I'll warrant, by her clothes and the way her mouth drops open at every new corner we turn.

I should do my bit to help her, as I would hope someone would help me if I were ever in a new city. I might have to escape to Amsterdam or France soon. I push this thought away.

London is a dangerous place if you don't know your way about. I'll help her quickly and then get on with my work.

'This is where you get water.' I point out the conduit and before I can stop her, she pushes forward to splash her face. She receives a heavy clout from a woman for getting in her way. A guard approaches and the girl backs off quickly.

'Where I come from, you are allowed water,' she utters ruefully.

'Here you must take your turn.' I nod to the line of people waiting.

She rubs fiercely at the back of her ear, as water dribbles from her chin. Her face, now only streaked with dirt, looks slightly more acceptable.

'It was so cold.' She shivers. 'But it was worth the pain.'

'Of the water, or the slap?'

'Both. I feel better and ready for adventure again.'

I tut. 'This way.'

Hiding my amusement, I hook myself into the path of the wind, letting its blast propel me along, drawing my cloak close about me. This girl's clothes are made of wool and leather – but they are not warm enough for her to survive the night outside. If I do not help her, who knows what will happen to her?

'What's your name?' she shouts at my back. Her voice mixes with that of a woman selling oranges and she calls more loudly, as if I have not heard her. When I don't answer, she begins to guess, yelling names as if she were selling them. 'Isabel? Catherine? Margery? Joan?'

This is a fine game at a fireside, but it does not suit the streets.

'Alice.' I toss my name over my shoulder. It chimes clear as a bell. It was my mother's name, and it makes me proud to tell it. I sidestep to avoid an oncoming carriage, feeling muck splatter my skirts.

'I'm Honesty,' she calls after me. 'It was the name of my mother's favourite flower.'

I stop and the girl almost bumps into me. Her mother must be gone too.

'It is a good name.'

'Thank you. Alice is beautiful. Like honey dripping from a summer-day hive and making the grass glossy.'

A strange description but pleasing, nonetheless. We smile at each other.

Honesty says, 'Once, I tied animal bones to the soles of my shoes for night skating under a waxing moon, but I was chased by baying wolves.'

I *tsk* and hurry along.

'Howling, they set after me, their claws scarring the frozen surface. Little did they know that they were weakening the ice with their scratches, making it easy for the water to seep through. They drowned, all of them, yowling and scrabbling and screaming to the unforgiving skies.'

'Can wolves scream?' I know they cannot.

'When you have stolen their dinner for skating, they can.' Honesty rubs her arms. 'It is much colder here than where I came from. I wish I had not washed my face. The dirt was helping to keep me warm.'

'Is it warm in Wales?' I snort because I do not suppose it is.

'No, not at all.' She giggles. 'I live close to the sea, and it is cold as a snowball on the nose at this time of year. The fish are frozen solid when they are caught. You can break them in two with your fingers. Snap.'

I laugh again. It is preposterous.

'Once the whole town froze and the buildings became so covered in ice, they all slid into the sea.'

I laugh uncontrollably this time, which is not like me at all. Her stories have taken my mind off my own troubles and I am grateful for it.

There is a sudden surge of people, and we have to stand aside to let them pass.

'Where are they going in such a rush?' Honesty asks, squashing herself flat to a timbered wall.

'They are on their way to a hanging.'

'Oh, how awful.' She watches them pass. 'Can we go?'

'You do as you please. I don't have time for entertainment.'

She deliberates, then decides that saving her own life is more urgent than watching others lose theirs. We walk on.

'Is it much further?' She looks so tired I fear she could fall flat on her face in the dung.

'We will cross the bridge and I will leave you there.'

Her mouth drops open when she sees London Bridge and I feel a prickle of pride.

'It has houses on it?'

'Yes. And many shops.'

'Is it safe?' Honesty looks down at the brown river fearfully.

'What unusual questions you ask. We have the finest buildings in the world here.'

'It will take an hour to cross it.'

'Which is why we must make haste.'

Ducking a wonky candlemaker's sign, I nip between a group of sailors who spill out from an alehouse, singing, and a soldier crying into his beer. A couple of men stagger happily, drunk from too much wassailing.

When Honesty catches me, she is out of puff. 'You must ... be very important ... to be carrying ... a parcel for ... the Queen.'

I nod. No one ever asks me questions about my life, because I keep it as small as I can, and I can feel my tongue bursting to tell someone something, anything.

Honesty gawks, half-starved, at a baker's and I buy her a cake. I don't bother bartering for it, as time is running short. She eats it so quickly I fear she will choke.

'I live at Greenwich Palace,' I say proudly as

she scurries alongside me. It is true for now, at least.

'A palace? Are you a friend of the Queen?'

'No.' I check about me that no one has overheard. 'I work there. It is very important work. This way.'

We pass an apothecary's beaked masks and remedies on display, and I have to go back to take hold of Honesty's arm. She soon stops again to stare at a mercer draping rippling silk over his outstretched arm as if it is trickling water.

Honesty keeps talking as I drag her away. 'A palace must be magnificent. Are there turrets lined with gold? Do kings and princes from around the world visit often? I bet you get to do wonderful things.'

'I take care of the Queen's clothes. It's a very important job for someone of thirteen years.' I cannot help revelling in her astonishment. And why shouldn't I tell this girl a little of my life? No one else is interested. 'This is the very finest lace. Handcrafted in Southwark. I was fortunate enough to get work at the palace and now I am surrounded by beauty and riches.'

Her eyes shine and I find myself prattling

on. 'Have you seen rubies red as a robin's breast? Sapphires bluer than swallows? The Queen has so many. Furs and skins and enough velvet gowns to clothe a village. Her pearls are from oceans five fathoms deep. Her diamonds are as clear as a babe's tear and large as a goose's egg.'

I do not have her way with words, but I have tried and Honesty is suitably impressed. I am glad.

'What do you do there? With the clothes. Do you have lots of gowns yourself? Are you allowed to wear silver and gold? Do you actually know the Queen?'

'I am in a position of authority, treated well and yes, I have come very close to the Queen indeed.' I tell her of the processions we have been on across the country. How we pack the clothes and keep them, so the Queen may look glorious for her people in each new town. I tell her of the feasts and the dances, the festivities, frivolities and masked balls. By the time I stop, I have spoken more than I have to anyone in years. I almost believe I love the palace as much as I say I do.

A blast of bitterly cold air brings me back to my senses. The wind whistles past us, rattling my words along the bridge where they could be caught by anyone. I scold myself.

'I must hurry. The wigmaker will close soon. If you cross the bridge to the end and then turn along the river, you will find rooms at the Cross Keys Inn. I wish you safe journey and good fortune, Honesty.'

'Thank you, Alice. You are too kind.'

I go. I talked too much, and I must keep my guard.

I turn to make sure Honesty is not following me. She stands where I left her, waving me a hopeful farewell. I nod, then give a tight smile to show her we part as friends. The wind keens loudly enough to startle swans from the river as I leave.

I don't look back again. Being alone is the best way to survive.

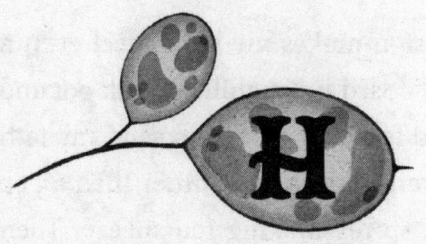

CHAPTER THREE

# HONESTY

'Fare thee well.' I call after Alice, watching her disappear, leaving me alone. As alone as you can be in this multitude of people. Continuing along the bridge in the direction she pointed, I consider myself lucky to have met such a wondrous girl on my very first day in London. How fortunate she is to be so important. I want to be that important. How is it possible to work at the palace? I jump over a rat the size of a cat and am jostled aside by swine, oinking and squealing. If I had not been so astounded by her tales, I would have asked her how she came by that work.

There are so many shops on the bridge, and I feel properly sorry for myself that I have so few coins. A glover's sign makes my hands feel even more cold. Another board has a quill and ink pot and I wonder if I could learn to write and send my father a letter of forgiveness. I pass a vintner then a pepperer, the tickle of spices making me sneeze. Then my nose discovers a stench so foul I can barely breathe. I look up.

There, ahead of me, is a huge gate with something on top of it. No, it cannot be. Heads. Severed human heads. On spikes. Some twenty or more. Gulls wheel and peck at them high above. It is a vision from my worst nightmare.

Someone shouts and I am thrown aside by a swerving wagon, landing on my knees in the sludge. Immediately a shopkeeper comes out and prods me with a broom to move along.

Never have I seen anything so disgusting or terrifying. What is this place? In my town I've seen public whippings and have thrown an egg or two at people locked in the stocks, but this is quite different. And all these people go happily about their business as if the heads are not there. I've heard stories of the things that happen to traitors if they betray the Queen but to see it…

I cannot survive here alone. I need a friend.

Running in the direction Alice went, I do not care if I bump into people. I must find her and make her help me. I know she was going to a wigmaker. Please, fortune, take pity on me.

Just as I am getting desperate, I spot her, by some miracle. Her curls, such a vibrant yellow, stretch to the sky. Her goodbye, and the speed with which she left, tell me that she did not want me as a companion for this part of her journey. I'll follow her to the palace and plead with her there, where I will be harder to refuse.

From a safe distance, I watch as Alice makes her collection and, wrapping herself more tightly than her latest package, ventures back into the cold. I follow her, taking care not to get too close. She goes down the riverbank and gets into a barge. I get into the same barge, close behind. I do not want to travel any further – I am weary and need sleep – but my quest is taking me along the Thames. Perhaps I shall meet the Queen herself and she will give me one of those dresses of velvet and gold. I laugh loudly. Everyone in London is too busy to notice. I could somersault into the river and get barely more than a glance.

The boatman takes the remainder of my money

and I sit at the back. I can see Alice ahead of me, but there are many other people between us and I keep my head low in case she turns. The familiar pull of the water beneath me reminds me of home. I close my heart to it. I can't look back – I have escaped.

Our boat has to fight for our space on the water. The cake churns in my stomach with the sway of the tide. Clutching hard, I try to adjust to the bounce and heave of the current. The motion feels so different to the sea. Not even close to that lapping, bobbing comfort, like a swaddled babe rocking to sleep. I will learn to love it.

When we pass the Tower of London, the oarsmen point it out, a foreboding hulk where so many are imprisoned. Then Traitor's Gate.

Horrified, I see people chained to the banks of the river. To be punished? For what? Will they be drowned with the tide? How cruel this world can be. What an exciting place London is. A wizened old man leans from our barge and shouts, 'Criminals,' with such vehemence he almost topples in. I look ahead to see if Alice is upset by the sight of those left to die, but she, like everyone else, seems to think it normal.

I study the boats we pass. Some are laden with barrels, just like the ships that come into the harbour in my hometown are. All that food, sitting there, if I reached out, but I've heard what they do to thieves. Now I've seen what they do to traitors, I worry it's dangerous for me to follow Alice to the Queen. And yet I am no traitor, and Alice is my only hope, now that my last coins are spent.

I am between a woman with a mewling babe and a man who seems to know a great deal about everything and has a greater need to tell everyone.

'Would you look at that!' He points at a boat carrying screeching animals.

'What are they?' I ask.

'Monkeys, of course!' He guffaws. 'She doesn't know what a monkey is!' He nudges the woman with the baby, who pointedly ignores him. The baby grizzles at his sour breath.

'I know what they are. I have just never seen one in real life,' I tell him sullenly, making him laugh even harder.

The monkeys show me their teeth, as if they are laughing too. One reaches beyond his crate and tries to steal a bird from a cage. He narrowly misses but causes a flurry of red feathers and alarmed cheeps.

'They lost a tiger overboard last night,' the man warns, leaning close so I can see remnants of pease pudding in his beard. 'I presume you know what a tiger is?' He puts his filthy hands up like claws and roars. 'Just wanted to warn you because tigers are born to swim.'

I shuffle away from the side of the boat, and he laughs at me so hard his hat tips off. I resist the temptation to knock it overboard and search the water for tell-tale tiger teeth.

The air is foul and thick, fish guts and scum. I can still smell the coal I nestled next to on the boat leaving Dinbych-y-Pysgod. The thick mud on my shoes from Bristol. The stagecoaches, then the carts. What a journey I have been on. I am dog-tired. I close my eyes.

When I open them again, the explaining man has found a new victim. The crick in my neck says I have been asleep. The light is sea-silver bright, and squinting, I gasp loudly. We are sliding close to a building of such pomp I can barely believe it is real. Blinking, I sit up straight.

'Is this Greenwich?' I interrupt the man who knows everything.

'It is.' He turns to me briefly. By the time he turns back to the woman, she has taken the opportunity to pretend she is kipping.

'And that, the palace?'

'What else should it be?' he sulks.

I see Alice ascend the bank then clamber off after her. Nerves and the cruel wind make my teeth chatter. Afraid of ending up in the water, I take too long and lose sight of my quarry. She must have gone into the palace. I have missed my chance to convince her to find me work.

Crouching by a bush for shelter, I pretend I am not afraid. I must play my part: a courageous girl who can take care of herself, not a frightened, poor wretch who will starve to death in the shadows of the palace or be set upon by murderers. My hands tremble with cold and worry. I must keep moving.

The palace is directly on the river, so I pace about, watching the comings and goings, hoping to catch sight of Alice in one of the hundred windows or among the stream of people at the gates. I start at each snap of a flag caught up by the gale, each candle lit or curtain drawn. Alice is nowhere to be seen and the day will fail soon. My heart thuds painfully. Being here after dark will not make a merry tale. I must take charge of my own story once more, but how?

I shall talk my way in somehow. It takes

every bit of courage I can muster to approach the entrance to the courtyard. I practise what I shall say to the guard. *I am Honesty. I come in search of good employment. I am a hard worker and...*

Startled by a loud barking, I stop still. There are shouts and trumpets and hounds. Even more people gather, as if from nowhere. My lower jaw clanks open. It is the Queen! She is surrounded by lords and servants and ladies-in-waiting and draws a babbling crowd around her immediately.

I am overawed and rooted to the spot, then forget my worries and hurry to join them. We follow her across the meadow. We're all talking exuberantly because we are sky-high. People kneel and take off their hats as she passes, then join the river of us in her wake.

She stops and we stop. We goggle as she holds out her hand to a groom for a bow and arrow, then tests the wind's direction. On such a blustery day, she obviously does this to get a laugh. This is why people love her. With an expert aim, she fires into a target held up by a brave and stupid man. Our hurrahs scare the pigeons from the grass.

I gawp and laugh and jump up and down. I cannot help myself. To come this close to the

Queen. I, Honesty, a girl from Wales, can see how her hair sings the orange joy of autumn leaves. At her throat jewels catch the light. Her face is powerful and frightening and brilliant. Her teeth are black as the sea at night, where she has some, her face white as newly squeezed milk, her eyes ferocious. I cannot look at them for fear. The part of her gown not hidden beneath her cloak is white as a cloud with gold stars twinkling and stitched with silver thread.

We watch and cheer again and again as arrows hunt out their target. There has never been a more magnificent moment than this in the history of the world. The crowd has grown to such a number I have to use my well-practiced elbows to dart to the front so that I may see her better. If I held out my hand, I could almost touch her.

My nostrils twitch, alert to the scent of danger, that strange taste of coppery blood on my tongue. I scan the crowd. People smiling and cheering. Faces raised to watch the rainbow path of a misfired arrow. Except one. A man. His expression solid and mean. He is too still. I sense something rotten. He puts his hand beneath his leather jerkin, I catch the dull glint of metal.

'No!' I shout and run towards the Queen.

The attacker rushes at her, his dagger held high. The day is drowning, and my legs are made of water, but I stand in his way.

I feel a thump of something on my shoulder and crumple to the ground with the attacker beneath me. I am pulled back hard and tossed aside. There is a scuffle and screams as the man is dragged away. The Queen is surrounded by guards, and I am left on the wet grass, forgotten and almost trampled.

Dazed, I pull myself up to my knees. I can hear the Queen continuing with her archery. Cheers again from the crowd. Through their legs, I see her testing an arrow and missing her target completely. She holds a hand up for silence, and comments on how its direction has been spoiled by the taint of treachery and it is not flying as straight as it should. She laughs. Everyone laughs. I was almost murdered and now I am ignored.

My legs shaking, I stand. At once, the Queen turns to me, her fiery eyes pinning me to the spot. My breath flutters in my throat and though I try to speak to beg forgiveness, I don't know why, I cannot.

She beckons me closer, and I go. What choice do I have with a hundred watchers?

'Who are you, girl?'

She spoke to me. I am struck dumb. Someone raps the back of my head.

'Honesty.' I'm not certain how you address a queen. 'Your Majesty,' I try hastily, seeing my head on a spike.

'You tremble and yet I am the one who has barely kept my life.' Roaring with laughter, she sets the crowd off again. Her leather-gloved hand hushes them.

'How do you come to be here, saving the life of the Queen?'

Stories flash through my mind. I think to lie to the Queen would be a very bad start indeed. 'I want to work at the palace, Your Majesty.'

The day lays heavy on my shoulders, a city of eyes upon me. Trembling, I spin a story quickly in my mind to comfort me as I wait, about a girl who lives at the palace and has everything she wants.

'Well, honest Honesty, I must give you just rewards for saving my life.'

My ears prick up at the word 'rewards'.

The Queen takes off her glove to show her

beautiful hand then raises it to beckon one of her ladies-in-waiting. I step back as her expression instructs me. Without looking at me again, she takes her leave, a baaing flock of people behind her, scattering swans. Only the lady-in-waiting remains.

She stares at me awhile. She has a chained squirrel on her arm, and it stares at me too, its tail twitching. I wait uncertainly.

'Who are you?'

This irritates me because I have already told the Queen. Why should I answer to this woman? I remember my position. 'My name is Honesty.'

'Is it?' She looks me up and down. 'And how can we be sure that you were not here to be part of the attack?' I gasp at that. 'I saved the Queen's life.'

My exclamation makes her smirk and I squirm with irritation.

'Did you now?'

I can tell from her tone that she is doubtful but resist the urge to keep protesting my innocence. Sometimes, protesting too much can make you seem guilty.

'Where are you from?'

'Wales.'

She rolls her eyes. 'That much, I can tell.'

'The west. A town called Dinbych-y-Pysgod.'

'I've never heard of it.'

Her voice is reedy and disinterested. 'The Queen says you are to work and live at the palace.'

My knees almost give way with shock. The lady doesn't seem to notice, as she feeds the squirrel a nut.

'I don't suppose you know what that means for you, girl?'

I shake my head and wonder.

'I do not trust you, girl. We will be keeping a close watch on you, won't we, Puck?' She pets the squirrel. My position is lower than a rat with a bushy tail.

I wish I was able to defend myself but the whispers of night start to purple the sky and there is no way I will say anything to jeopardise a chance of life at the palace. I will not tell her how she looks like a horse I once knew.

This day has been long and my legs give way beneath me. Someone catches me from behind and supports me. It is Alice.

'Honesty is my friend,' she states, to both the lady's and my astonishment.

'Yes, I am Alice's friend,' I hear myself saying from somewhere far away. 'Will we be working together?'

'For all I care.' The lady whinnies her disgust, nostrils flaring. Her contempt makes my temper flicker, but it's overwhelmed by another feeling. Excitement.

'Show her to her duties. Be quick about it.' She looks at me as though I were a leech. 'You do as you are told.'

'Yes, miss.' I try a curtsey, but my knees are weak.

'You have much to learn.' She walks off, indignant and impressive, leaving the delicate scent of lavender behind her for a moment before the river barges in with its mouldy stench again. I try to take in all that just happened.

'How did you get here?' Alice prods my arm.

'Fate brought me to you.'

'Hmm.' She purses her lips, and I know she thinks I'm lying. 'The Queen has never even noticed me, and you turn up and have spoken to her on your first day.'

'Fortune smiles upon me.' I try out my best lucky face and hope that she won't slap it.

'It will be wonderful to welcome another stray to the palace, I'm certain.'

She doesn't look certain at all.

I wince as pain throbs in my shoulder and Alice quickly checks that I'm not bleeding. I know that there have been attempts to kill the Queen before. Some people do not think we should follow her religion. Some do not think that she should be queen at all.

'This way, Honesty. Follow me.' Her examination over, Alice leads the way.

I follow, my shoulder aching from the attack and the rest of my body aching from the everything else.

This is where my life begins. Here on this coldest of days with the pinch of incoming night on my cheeks, raging hunger in my gut, and the old me flowing out with the corpses of tigers on the tide.

## CHAPTER FOUR
# ALICE

Honesty tags behind again. My breath is only now coming back, after the attempt on the Queen's life. How different my own life would be now if that man had succeeded. His screams still ring in my ears.

I show Honesty into the palace grounds. Torches are being lit to fend off the dark and the windows glow.

Honesty has followed me here, of that I have no doubt. Now she will see that some of the things I told her earlier were not entirely the truth. Walking briskly, I take her through a small door, along a warren of passages that can only be navigated by someone who knows the palace well.

It isn't that I want her to lose her way, just that I want her to see how well I know mine.

'You are to behave yourself here.' I make my voice strict. 'We report to Maude and she will have no slacking.'

I don't even get a response. Honesty is too busy drinking everything in. I lead her past huge timber doors, through cavernous rooms, lead-paned windows crisscrossing the light as we walk.

Outside the kitchens, feathers fly up as chickens are beheaded and plucked. Those still living, held nearby in boxes, squawk and cluck the alarm. I take Honesty to the door and watch her enjoying the blast of heat from the many fires and steaming pots and cauldrons. Gawping at the piles of pies, she licks her lips, then sniffs wishfully at the aroma of baking bread.

'Wait here.' I tell her, then go in, just through the door, to get the attention of one of the boys.

I bid him fetch us some ale and slug a tankard back myself while Honesty downs hers.

'The fireplace is taller than my head.' Honesty splutters in awe. 'There is a whole hog upon it.'

I glance at the boar spinning on a spit and see Barnaby is pretending to turn it, though actually doing nothing. A dog running on a wheel inside the turnspit is really powering it round and round.

Barnaby pretends to be enthralled by the black soot on the chimney breast, but I keep clicking my fingers at him till he can no longer ignore me and tell him to come with us. I take a mutton pie and give it to Honesty, looking away as she gollops it down ravenously. That is a hunger I have seen too often.

'This way.' Taking the lead, I let them follow me.

'What is your name?' Barnaby is not shy of anyone.

Honesty cannot speak for chewing.

'Her name is Honesty.'

'Ha!'

I tut at him, the cheeky little sprite, but something inside me is pleased that he laughed at her name, so I do not clip his ear.

'You'll show her some respect.' I push on ahead, winding this way and that.

'This is the undercroft,' I tell Honesty, who is picking the last crumbs of pastry off her cloak and licking them from her fingers. 'The serving hatch is here. This is where you collect your meals.'

She nods enthusiastically, and I think again of how lucky we are to have food and shelter so easily at the palace and how I cannot help but be grateful to the Queen, no matter what anyone else says.

Maude appears suddenly, as always, as if she is formed from shadows.

'What are you doing dawdling here, Alice? Who is this?'

'This is Honesty.'

'Honesty? By name and nature? We'll see about that.' Maude glares beyond us at two of the young servants, who are daring to have fun. She hastens after them, leaving her cold presence behind her.

'You must listen keenly when Maude gives you orders, or she will box your ears.'

Honesty rubs her ears and I know that they have known boxing before.

I carry on. 'Here, the cellars.' Noises of hammering echo out. Down there the barrels are rolled and corked. I shudder to think of the underground tunnels beneath us, dark and icy and swallowing. I stay away from them as much as I can.

Barnaby is spooked by none of it. 'Where are you from, Honesty?'

I let him carry on, inquisitive imp.

'Wales,' Honesty says, looking back at the kitchens with longing.

'I hear it is a land of grass and not much else.'

I let him goad her a little.

'Do you have houses there?' he asks with a laugh.

'It is a land of extreme beauty. Deep lush valleys and magnificent mountains. I live in a...' There is a pause, giving away that she is hiding something. '...very large house.'

Her face has reddened with anger or embarrassment. I cannot tell which.

'We have fine rivers and glorious seas, castles and a harbour to rival Bristol. Our people are poets and storytellers the like of which the world has never known.'

'Do you ever tell lies, Honesty?' Barnaby asks, then runs ahead chuckling. He is eight or nine, I would think, but grown up at the court too quickly and seen too much.

His shock of red hair is matched by the shade of Honesty's cheeks as she blows them out. She makes a quick show of chasing him, but is quickly out of puff. I notice that she does not deny the lies, which is interesting.

'This palace ... is ... like a town in ... itself,' she manages as we pass the chapel. 'It is truly enormous.'

I stop to straighten a tapestry patterned with storks, newly hung for the Queen's arrival then take a wrong turn purposely, calling Barnaby to follow, so she can see the courtyard with the fountain at its centre. I delight in her sigh at its beauty. Lit gold by the torchlight, it chatters richly.

'When it gets colder, the water freezes in that shape. A crown of ice.'

'It gets colder than this?'

'Sometimes the Thames freezes over entirely.'

A group of men are throwing horseshoes at a target. Barnaby comes close, waits until the men shout loudly at a successful hit and speaks, using the noise so nobody hears him but us. 'If it freezes this year, the ghost of King Henry will sleigh up the river from Hampton Court to chop off your head.'

I clip him hard this time. This kind of teasing is dangerous, and the walls have ears here. Barnaby, at his age, should know not to joke about royalty, alive or dead.

He yips in pain, then pokes his tongue at us. That boy will get himself in trouble.

Honesty bathes in the light pouring in through the courtyard garden. The cloisters are gilded gold.

'Where are we going, Alice?'

'Here.' Barnaby calls joyfully, skipping ahead down a passageway and opening a door. 'My lady.' He chortles as he leads Honesty in. 'Alice says you are to be cleaned. I can smell why.'

'Fetch a kirtle dress for Honesty, please, Barnaby, and keep your mischief to yourself.'

Holding his freckled nose between his finger and thumb, he scampers off, giggles ribboning behind him as he dodges between servants, lords and ladies. They bend out of his way like reeds at a riverbank.

'He listens to everyone's conversations, but none of their manners,' I tell Honesty, who looks downcast by her own stink.

I draw her into the room and try not to laugh at her startled expression as Esther, one of the other maids, pours hot water into a tub. 'Take your clothes off behind the screen.'

Honesty holds her disgusting clothes more closely to her body. I watch as she backs away from the open fire and the water warming on it.

Esther mocks her. 'Haven't you never had a bath before?'

'Thank you, Esther. That will be all.' I'm glad to dismiss her for she is a sour puss and almost always unkind.

Once she's gone, which takes a while as Esther pulls many faces at my giving her orders, I turn back to Honesty with determination. 'You needn't be afraid. You will not drown.'

She takes a couple of timid steps towards the tub. 'The water is hot?'

'Of course it is.' This should be obvious from the wisps of steam curling in the air.

'I will boil like a sea snail in a pot.'

'It's not that hot. See?' I put my hand in to show her, trailing my fingers, caressing the surface and making eddies and whirls. 'Trust me, Honesty.'

She does.

Barnaby reappears at the door as Honesty retreats behind the wooden screen to remove her filthy dress. When it drops to the floor, I bid her kick it to me so that I can pass it to him to burn.

'It is the only one I have.'

'It is beyond saving,' I state gently.

'Covered with fleas from all the Welsh sheep.' Barnaby snorts as I usher him out. He hops as if he were a flea himself and we hear, 'Ouch, ouch,

ouch,' fading away as he pretends he is being bitten.

'Come on then. In you get.'

I can see Honesty peeking warily through the patterned holes cut in the wood. Eventually she creeps out, wrapped in a linen towel.

'If you want to work at the palace, the first step is to be clean. We can't have Queen Elizabeth's visitors thinking that she doesn't look after her maids now, can we?'

I turn away, suppressing my laughter as she whines like a frightened pup, then gasps as she dips a toe in. I can hear slopping as she climbs into the tub, and finally a satisfied sigh at the warmth of it.

'Are you in properly?'

'I am,' she declares, with such pride at her achievement.

I turn back to her and see a bruise ripening on her shoulder from the attack. I give her a herb poultice to press on to it.

'Now let's get you clean.'

I scrub her until the water is grey with the filth of London and Wales and everywhere in between and then I help her out.

'Your first-ever bath. It wasn't so terrifying, was it?'

'I will never have one again.' Shivering now, as her skin cools, Honesty examines her wrinkled fingertips. She has forgotten the joy of wallowing already.

I move her closer to the fire then help her to get dry. Once she is warm again and smiling, I stand her in front of a looking glass. I enjoy hearing her surprise as she sees herself. She is completely free of grime. Her skin gleams and her hair shines, chestnut-brown in the light.

Pointing her to a bowl and a jug, I give her sugar to clean her teeth. Then I comb her hair so that it will shine even more. When I am done, I let her admire herself again, standing behind her so that I too am reflected in the glass.

'I look like a new girl,' she states.

'As of today, you are.'

'I smell like blossoms and oranges.'

'Myrtle and lavender.' I roll my pomander between my fingertips. I wear it always hanging from my waist. The familiar patterns of the metal ball press memories into my skin.

'What's that?'

I hadn't meant for it to catch Honesty's attention, but there is no shame in it. 'It belonged to my mother. She loved it. You can fill it with different flowers whatever the time of year. I…'

My voice catches in my throat. I am quiet by nature and this girl seems to understand that and is kind with it. She nods and lets me be silent.

'May I?'

Honesty reaches out and though I've never let anyone touch the pomander before, I see no reason why she shouldn't. It is tied to the cord at my waist, so I can still pull it back. She runs her finger over the intricate pattern of metal. The whorls and hearts twist and twine. My mother found it on the banks of the Thames and brought it home to clean. It is so full of my love for her.

'It is truly handsome,' Honesty murmurs.

I want to say something, but I can't find big enough words.

'My mother.' Honesty studies the pomander closely. 'My mother too.'

We both follow the markings on it with our fingertips.

There is a knock at the door and Barnaby puts his head through before he is invited. He is always quick to come back when he isn't needed. Honesty dashes behind the screen and I chide him for his rudeness. 'You should always wait when a lady is dressing.'

'I don't see any ladies here.'

I swing for him, but he ducks my slap, then goes to crouch by the fire, spitting in it for luck, and making the flames crackle. I wait, listening to Honesty humming a tune as she dresses. It is a song about someone with green sleeves. It is a popular song here too, though I doubt it will last. Songs come and go like seasons nowadays.

When Honesty shows herself, Barnaby hoots in astonishment. 'Where is she? The girl I brought in? She is not here, is she?'

He is a cheeky little rascal, but we both laugh.

'Honesty, a true lady, and defender of the Queen and the realm,' he announces, throwing linen towels over the puddles of water on the floor so that she might not get her feet wet.

'You can pick those up,' I instruct him, but he runs off giggling down the passageway again so we have to retrieve them. 'Off to do mischief elsewhere, of that I have no doubt.'

Finally, when everything has been tidied, I inspect Honesty.

She tries out a new haughty face to match her clean clothes.

'You'll do well.' I confirm. 'Now I must show you your duties.'

I lead the way past many chambers, each with something for Honesty to be distracted by. Guards, all of whom she introduces herself to, let us through the doors. We make very slow progress.

'Is everyone always this busy?' she asks, as grooms and maids scuttle past with candlesticks and beeswax candles.

'There is always plenty of work to do but the Queen is planning a celebration for Twelfth Night.'

I take a deep breath, realising how near that day is. I am afraid. Honesty is too caught up in the glitter of the things being carried past us to notice.

We are lucky to be treated so well here, but Father tells me it is so that people will not think badly of the Queen. If she is able to treat every groom and maid so well she will seem to have overwhelming riches and power. Many of those outside the palace walls have it worse, far worse, and I have been told that I must keep them in my heart.

'Do we get to go to the party?' Honesty asks, spinning around in front of a wall painted blue with golden stars so she looks like she is flying.

'No. Only the men serve. Our work will be done by then.'

I do not add that it is possible to hide and watch it all, because I do not want her to see what will happen. I do not want her to witness another attempt on the Queen's life. To guess that I was a part of the plot.

Honesty is deflated and stops momentarily, before taking flight again. 'The festivals in Wales are so exciting. Every midsummer, our whole town dances around a maypole. Last year we danced for so long, our feet wore a circle in the grass and the moon lit the path of our footsteps like a silver moat around our ribboned tower.'

'That sounds wonderful.' I love how her stories lift me from my own life. They take me out of my skin and let me float above myself. 'I wish I could go to a celebration like that.'

'You will, Alice. We will go together one day.' She is so exuberant, full of life. 'Even at this Twelfth Night party, we will listen for the music and sneak a dance.' She skips with joy.

I imagine it now. To dance and laugh and swing each other about by our hands. But I put thoughts of happiness out of my mind: this party will not be a chance for celebration.

'Are we heading for the Queen's wardrobe?' Honesty asks.

We move out of the way for some men, who strut like peacocks in their doublets and hose, plumes in their hats, all competing to have the widest ruffs.

'No. The mistress of the robes and the ladies-in-waiting are the only ones allowed.'

'Oh.' She is disappointed but quickly brightens, as seems to be her way. 'Describe the gowns to me instead. You have worked with them, haven't you? And I can picture things most excellently.'

I list them. Skirts of silk and bodices of velvet, all studded with pearls and jewels, all elaborately embroidered. Ruffs as big as serving plates and of such fine lace they could have been woven by spiders.

'The softest furs from the deep forests of Russia.' I say as if I have journeyed there myself. 'Satins and silks. Materials from Venice and India.'

'I can see them.' Honesty stands in the middle of the passageway with her eyes closed. Servants have to go around her, some of them baffled by her, others mocking. 'How they dance like raindrops in a soft spring shower. And shimmer like the path of a full moon on the sea.'

I pull at her elbow. She continues as we walk. Is she ever quiet?

'Once I followed the moon path across the waves. It led me to an island where folk as small as candles lived. They drank bladderwrack and glasswort wine from seashells and played pipes made of barnacles. Festive little folk they were. They frolicked all night by the light of fireflies and kept me jigging to their music till my feet were sore.' She jigs a little to demonstrate. 'No matter how I tried to rest, I could not, my feet continued to dance until they bled, for the melody they were playing had charmed me and as the dawn broke, the island began to sink into the sea.'

She barely pauses for breath, and I wonder if she talks as she sleeps too.

'They were creatures that could survive underwater, but I, being a mortal soul, was soon swimming for my life. It was lucky that a passing fisherman reeled me in, thinking me an exceedingly fat fish.'

Keeping ahead, so she cannot see how my cheeks

burn, I lead the way to the laundry room. In my description of my life at the palace when I first met her, I left this bit out. I concentrate on the slap of my footsteps, feeling my insides squirm. 'Do you keep a single thought in your head without expressing it?'

'How can I not speak? Look at the way the panels are carved with grapes.'

'Yes, I have seen them.'

'Have you noticed how the ceilings are painted with cherubs and clouds?'

'I have.'

She stops at every window to look out. 'Oh, how the gardens make my heart sing. Look at the ponds, how they glitter in the flames from the braziers. They are as big as lakes, and the statues, there are so many of them. How I should like to be a statue and live in those glorious gardens. And what's that?'

She points to the clock tower in the courtyard beneath the Great Hall. Purple and gold, it shines to show itself off in the flickering torchlight.

I tell her, 'It is a clock to tell the tides. So that the royal barge may travel more quickly to London.'

'I can hardly believe it.' She shakes her head. 'Look at the way the faces are carved into stone…'

My head begins to throb.

Eventually, we get to the room where we collect the washing. The stench brings tears to your eyes, and now, finally, she is quiet.

'Oh,' she says. 'Oh.'

Stacks of soiled garments are piled waist-high already, thanks to the number of people here for Christmastide.

'Oh,' Honesty repeats. For what else is there to say?

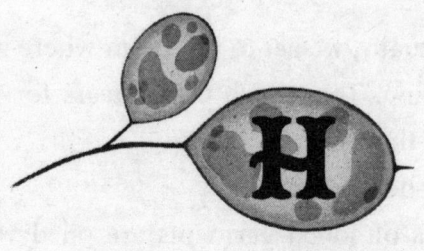

## CHAPTER FIVE
# HONESTY

I awake from a dream of dragons in dresses soaring above the Tower of London, breathing fire at me as I run to escape. At first, I don't know where I am. The ceiling is high, like a cathedral, and not the dark, small space we have at home.

Hearing a groan, I turn on my pallet to see Alice kneeling on hers, gripping her stomach in pain. Everything comes back to me. I am at the palace. I am at the palace. Alice is ill but I am at the palace.

'Alice, are you well?'

She wipes her mouth with the back of her hand. 'I do not know what ails me, Honesty. My stomach gripes.' She groans again, a little more loudly this time.

I am wary of sick people, but Alice does not appear to have a fever. There is no sheen of sweat on her skin and I cannot see any spots.

We have slept in the hall with about a hundred other servants and maids, most are already up and about and the hall which was littered with sleepers is now emptying fast. I help Alice to stand and carry her pallet and mine to where they are stored through the day. We go to eat our breakfast, eggs, butter and bread, then get our orders from Maude whose face is sleep-creased and already angry. Then we make our way through the labyrinthine passages to begin our work. Close to the chapel, Alice bends over double, sweat beading her brow.

'Can I get something to make you better?' She really does look sick.

'Go to collect the washing, but if you could very quickly get me some ginger from the kitchens, it would help settle me. Shall I ask somebody to show you the way?'

'Tell me, I will remember. Once I remembered a shopping list eight furlongs long. It began with cockles and flour, cinnamon and raisins...'

Alice groans loudly, and I remember that she needs my help. She tells me how to get back to the kitchens and I repeat it by rote while I support her to the privy. Checking there is plenty of hay for her to clean herself, I gladly leave her and the stink behind.

This is exciting. I follow her instructions, peeking into the rooms I pass and pretending to know where I'm going whenever anyone passes me. There are so many people rushing with garlands to decorate the palace for Twelfth Night, it is easy to wander without attracting much attention, though I am spiked in the arm by a gigantic wreath of holly as it is carried past.

Paintings of old kings stare down, their eyes following me, and tapestries make my mind roam to woods and battlefields. This palace is twenty times the size of the town where I was born, and I have only seen a part of it. The Queen's apartments are private, of course, and I can only imagine what riches lie there. The intricate ironwork stair-rails throw lace shadows onto the floor and I play them with my fingers until someone comes along and I recall my errand.

Eventually, after a couple of wrong turns, I come to a small enclosed garden. The kitchens must be nearby, but I'll just have a little look here, because at home we use plants to make us feel better.

It is neatly set out in squares with paths between and I find parsley, thyme and rosemary growing closely together. I bend to pick some. Straightening up, I see a girl of about seven or eight years, watching me.

'Hello. My name is Honesty.' I smile. 'What's yours?'

She shrugs and I wonder if she doesn't trust me enough to tell me. She clutches a doll in her hand.

'What is her name?' I ask.

'Janet,' she gives up shyly.

'She's beautiful. Do you live here in this garden?'

The girl very seriously shakes her head.

'Oh, that is a shame. I am searching for my most treasured possession. It was stolen from me by faerie folk.' Her eyes widen. 'If I tell you what I seek, will you help me?'

It is perishing and our breath whitens the space between us, but a story warms the coldest heart, and she seems keen to hear it.

'I'll begin one winter's night many years ago.'

I walk as I start to unreel my story. I have no idea where it will end. This is the greatest pleasure of it.

'The moon was but a sliver and I, being in a garden like this one, had no idea that I was being watched by faerie folk.' I watch her expression change from fear to astonishment.

'As you know,' I continue, looking about me for inspiration, 'the wee folk hide in herb gardens such as this.'

She nods and I smile. 'The night before, an evil faerie had stolen a human baby and replaced it with a changeling faerie child and now they had come back because they wanted more.'

I am starting to draw other listeners and this makes me flamboyant, projecting my voice theatrically so that it bounces from the stone and changing my posture to suit the different characters. 'I, being the bravest and the cleverest in our town, was put on watch and by singing a song so beautiful, I caught a faerie, one of the youngest and most foolish, as it could not help but come closer to hear.'

The girl comes closer to me.

'I held the faerie child prisoner. I had no

intention of doing it harm, you understand? I just wanted to use it for bargaining.'

The small girl chews at the skin around her fingers.

'And bargain I did. With the faerie child as bait, the other faeries showed themselves. Little did I know before, but the faerie child I held was that of the Faerie Queen's.'

She gasps. 'I had the changeling in a basket at my side and took it out to show them it was safe. I knew it was the faerie babe for a beard had begun to grow on its chin.'

There are a few laughs at this. The gardeners rest their hands and some of the servants have left their chores and come outside. I explain how the faerie folk gave the child back and promised to leave us in peace forever to cheers from the listeners, mixed with a few dubious expressions, for some think faeries too evil to include in stories. Seeing a feather on the ground, I add to my tale, telling the girl that they gave me a magical bird, which would always bring its owner courage, as part of the bargain.

'That is what I am seeking. I am afraid the faeries must have stolen it back or it must have flown away. But, no matter, because if you ever find a feather floating close to you, it means that the bird has brought you bravery.'

I pretend to hunt about again and she, not realising that she is being led, sees the feather and catches it gently as though it were made of magic, holding it out to me between finger and thumb.

'You have found one!' I say. 'No, I must not take it, for the feather is meant for the finder and is yours.'

She proudly shows it to Janet.

'Oh, and I forgot to say, if you lose the feather, it does not matter, for the courage lasts forever once you have it.'

It is a good story and I wait for praise but when I look round people are hurrying away from me as though I carry the plague. One sweeps the little girl into her arms and takes her in, Janet watching me from her dangling hand. Some of the servants look upwards, bow their heads and dash off. Soon I am left with the gardeners, working frenziedly about me. What went wrong?

I glance up and my body turns to stone. There at one of the windows is the Queen, watching me telling stories when I should be at work. I am done for.

I run into the palace, my thoughts rushing faster than my feet. I should have listened to Alice and gone to fetch the ginger. I will be thrown out. I will be tossed into the Thames, imprisoned in the Tower, tortured on the rack.

I can barely breathe by the time I find Alice and tears stream down my face. She is, thankfully, away from the latrines and looks a little better.

'Honesty, what is it?'

I pull her into a wood-panelled room, empty, and with no fire lit. My first instinct is to make up a story, but how will that help me now? I tell her everything. Every horrid, fearful, terrible detail plainly and truthfully. I see her expression change to horror.

'What do I do?' I cannot think, I am so scared. The winter's day waits at the window, grey and judgmental. I close my eyes. I will not be able to see the blue, yellow, black insides of my eyelids if my head is chopped off.

'Honesty.' Alice's voice falters. She clears her throat. 'I told you that you must obey orders. Why would you draw attention to yourself like this? We must always do as we are told.'

A sound at the door makes us both halt. I see my fear reflected in Alice's face. I scrabble to the window to escape. Every type of torture fills my mind. The scold's bridle: my head in a cage to stop me telling stories. The ducking stool, dunked over and over into the river. If I drown, they will forgive me but if I live, they will think me a witch and then I'll be hanged. I would rather fall to my death from this window than suffer any of these things.

'You, girl.'

I am too late. I turn to the lady with the horse face and flaring nostrils. Barnaby, who has clearly led her to me, peers from behind her, the sneaky little scullion.

'You, girl, are to come with me.'

Alice stands, her head bowed as though in prayer. I hear a bell knell from somewhere far away. My knees quake.

'Fare thee well, Alice.' I reach out and press my hands to hers. 'Thank you for everything.'

'Be quick about you,' the woman huffs.

I go, slowly, dragging my feet and trying not to whimper.

'It seems you have made quite the impression in your short time here, foiling assassination attempts and now with your *stories*.' The word 'stories' sounds like the worst kind of insult in her mouth.

'I did not mean to cause any harm. It was intended to entertain, not to offend.'

She snorts and gallops on ahead.

'What is to happen to me?' I plead, breaking into a trot and a sweat. I must do my best to face this with dignity. 'Am I to die?'

She brays with laughter. It is a cruel reaction.

'The Queen overheard your tale from the window.'

I hang my head in shame.

'Her Majesty is in deep melancholy today. She wants you to tell her a story to rouse her from this sadness.'

I snap my neck up. 'She wants me to tell her a story?'

'Do you need everything to be repeated to you?'

'No.' I run alongside her now so that I may be an equal in this race. 'Does she like stories? What kind would she like? Am I to make one up or tell her the same one again?'

'You may stop your gabbling for we are here.'

She clicks her fingers at me twice for silence. I enter a room so large and beautiful it is beyond the palaces of my imagination.

There, ahead of me, seated on a throne, magnificent and menacing, is Queen Elizabeth herself.

The ladies-in-waiting around her stop chattering and I am examined and appraised as I approach. I manage an inelegant curtsey which brings forth a ripple of laughter. Subdued, I clear my throat and wait to be told what to do.

'Girl. You are the same girl who saved my life, are you not?'

From somewhere inside my dragon heart, I find the wherewithal to speak. 'I am, Your Majesty.'

Again, I curtsey. With grace, this time.

'Your name escapes me. It is something about truth.'

I don't know whether I'm supposed to respond, but the silence echoes on for so long I say my name.

'Tell me a story, Honesty. And make it a good one, for I have no time for fools.'

The fool I saw playing the lute earlier sulks in a corner looking sorry for himself.

I try to think of a good story. My mind has gone blank. I stare at the tiles on the floor as I feel the Queen's eyes burn into my scalp.

'Have you lost your tongue, girl?'

My thoughts race, a cartwheel of ideas and pictures. I cannot bring to mind a single story. How people would mock me at home if they could see me. How Gwen Piggott would laugh. And there I have it. The stirrings of a story. I need to trust in my tale and begin.

'There was once an unfortunate girl called Gwen Piggott.' My words, shaky at first, become clearer and louder. More confident and full of colours. As if I was in the marketplace at home. I don't struggle with English for I have spoken it as well as Welsh my whole life. My mother said I entered the world talking. I picture the ladies-in-waiting in the clothes of my country and change their faces for the children of my town.

By the time I have finished the story of how Gwen Piggott was turned into a pig, I am surrounded by laughing ladies, who throw me trinkets, which I gather up gratefully.

The Queen, however, does not smile. She rests her elbow on her throne and supports her head with her hand. Have I bungled this? My hopes abandon me as I wait forlornly for my order of execution. I try to keep my gaze downcast, but I cannot help looking up. Eventually she raises her head an inch from the cradle of her palm.

'It is a good story,' she says, dismissing me with a gentle wave of her free hand.

I am led out on a cloud of hot air and happiness, my feet barely touching the earth.

I am Honesty. Storyteller to the Queen.

## CHAPTER SIX
# ALICE

I am wrung out with worry, my stomach roils again with nerves and threatens sickness. The fear which has made me so ill swells again inside me. When Honesty comes back to find me, I'm so relieved to see her alive that I fling my arms about her, though it is not usually my way to be so bold.

'Alice, you are squashing me.' She is muffled by my bonnet. 'Ouch. My shoulder.'

I let her loose. I had forgotten her injury and apologise, then watch in amazement as she empties her arms of exquisite treasures.

'What are these?' I fear the devil has taken hold of her, and she has stolen them. I listen as she babbles excitedly about how she was ordered to tell the Queen a story. How it was such a great success that the ladies-in-waiting all gave her gifts and how she got praise from the Queen herself. As she talks, I walk to the window and press my cheek to the lattice glass to cool it.

I have been with the Queen since I was ten years old and have received no special attention from anyone. I know that I must not look for recognition, but it might be nice to be thanked, noticed. To have gifts. To feel that someone was happy with me. Perhaps if that had ever happened for me, the path of my life would have altered. Perhaps I would have been able to make my own decisions and stay here, loyal to the Queen for the rest of my days.

I look out at the view of the river, and think how many tides I have observed, how many people sailing to new lands and freedom. Hot prickles of jealousy sting my neck and arms.

'Look, Alice. They gave me a bejewelled fan. It's painted with bulrushes and a kingfisher. Have you seen them? It's so delicate. Look how the jewels glister. I thought you might like to have it for your own?'

Turning from the window, I see Honesty holding it out to me. I cannot bring myself to take it when my thoughts are so angry. Trying to push the selfish envy deep down inside, I watch as Honesty places the fan in the willow basket where I keep my things. She mistakes my jealousy for modesty, I think. Presuming that I do not take it because I am kind and want her to have it.

I'm not certain I would have shared my spoils if I had been given such riches. But I have not been given anything, so I do not need to wonder what I would have done.

'Thank you.' It hurts my throat to say it.

'Even the squirrel enjoyed the story, I think.' She laughs. 'It jumped up and down on its chain.'

Perhaps I too could have been a friend of the ladies-in-waiting if I were not under such strict instructions to stay in the shadows. I have been sent here because I have always been as quiet as a dormouse and my father and brother think that I will slip by unnoticed. I wish that I could tell Honesty why I am really here. Perhaps she could help me? After only a moment's thought, I know she cannot.

'I wonder if it pulled at its chain because it hopes for escape. Or if it is happy to be kept – fed and stroked and imprisoned, listening to stories.'

I am not usually so outspoken. I don't know what it is about Honesty that brings my feelings so close to the surface.

'And this too.' Honesty puts an orange ribbon in next to the fan, and though I should feel grateful, anger still stirs in my gut. It is so unfair. To have to be grateful to her when she has only been here for such a small time.

'Thank you, Honesty. But I think we best get to our duties for the day now.' My harsh tone surprises me and her, but she covers it almost immediately.

'Oh, yes. Of course we must. We can share these things later.'

She is so eager to please me. I want to thank her for the gifts properly, but I know I would burst into tears, so I keep my counsel as we go to work.

Some of the others are there when we arrive at the laundry room and they are, as always, gossiping. Stories catch quicker than wildfire here.

'Here she is,' Amelia exclaims as Honesty dawdles in behind me.

'Ooh, tell us what happened with the Queen?' Marion dumps her dirty washing to listen. 'Did you actually speak to her? Did she speak to you?'

'We heard that you told her a story.' Barnaby is always around now, like an annoying gnat. I flap him away and pointedly start to gather up stinking garments.

'I did.' The gloat in Honesty's voice is clear and I chew the inside of my cheek. She sees my reaction. 'But I must get on with my work now.'

'Oh, please tell us. We can work at the same time,' Marion pleads. These girls have known me for years and now I am no more than a ghost.

'I cannot tell you the story that I told the Queen, since it was for her ears only,' Honesty says.

'Hers and the ladies-in-waiting and other servants present,' I correct, bristling and irritated.

'Ooh. Hark at her,' Barnaby exclaims and the others smirk.

'As Alice says…' Honesty puts her head to one side and tries to read my motives. 'I have told that story and, as you well know, stories, once told, are free to fly until they find their next teller. I have taken my turn with that tale and now it is someone else's.'

There is a collective moan. I busy myself with loading a sack, ignoring everyone's disgruntled faces. My reaction is not kind but there is something deep inside me, a maggot that wriggles, that resents Honesty's popularity. Why should she have so much when I have so little?

We fetch the key from the laundress for the high garden gate to the wash house, and I walk ahead so that I cannot see Honesty.

'Alice. Are you ill again?'

With supreme effort, I turn and smile and smile and smile, though I feel a villain. She seems to accept this.

'I shall tell you the story of the well maiden and the knight, if you like?'

I cannot resist and by the time we have reached the wash house she has captured me. The end of the story is so heart-breaking and hopeful, I sigh.

The others who have been listening set about their chores like clucking hens. As I crouch to scrub at a linen in the shallow channel of water, Honesty squats next to me and does the same.

'It truly is a remarkable tale,' I tell her, much as I hate to admit it. 'Thank you for sharing it with me.'

'Thank you, Alice, for listening. Perhaps you will tell me a story one day.'

'Perhaps.'

We work in silence, while the day spools out in chills and cawing crows.

Scrubbing these garments, I find I can also wash my bad thoughts away. I can forgive Honesty for her luck in getting an audience with the Queen. She has been so generous in sharing her gifts with me. The attention she has received will die down quickly enough, as all things do in the royal court. One fad is replaced by another, one fashion by the next. It is impossible to keep up with what is in favour or not. Honesty's success will soon turn to dust. I scrub and think how much I hate having to do this. Honesty works beside me, pulling faces of disgust at some of the stains. I must be kind to make up for my earlier spite.

'How did you learn to tell stories so eloquently?' I ask.

'My mother. She taught me the beauty of words as her mother taught her.'

We ponder this as we work. How words can lift the soul and take you anywhere. Just as I am about to tell her of my love of poetry, we are approached by one of the ladies-in-waiting. I believe her name is Helen, but we have never spoken.

I stagger as I stand because I have been bent

down for so long, then curtsey, my hands dripping water down my dress. She hides a vinegary face with a good deal of white paint and red lips.

'Come with me, Honesty. We want another story. The Queen has retired to her library alone and we need something jolly.'

'I have work I must finish,' Honesty says, struggling to her feet too.

'Ha! You may leave that and come with me, my sweet little pet.' She pats her on the head, and my fists clench.

Honesty looks to me and I bury my hands in my armpits, as if to warm them.

'We are nearly done here,' I say, though any idiot can see that it is not true.

As they leave, I feel ill thoughts wriggling inside me again. Getting back to work, I decide I must stay friends with Honesty however much it hurts. She was generous with her riches. As well as needing a friend, I may need more trinkets I can sell when I make my escape.

And as I wait for the awful event of Twelfth Night, her stories will be all that comfort me.

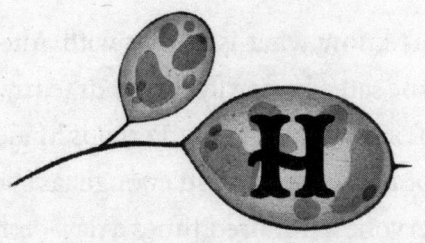

## CHAPTER SEVEN
# HONESTY

'I made up a tale about a girl who floated in on the Thames from the sea. Her song could change the direction of the tides, so the Queen's barge could travel quickly without the use of the tide clock. And she gave me payment for my story. Can you believe my luck, Alice? I will share the monies with you, of course.' I beam at people walking past London Bridge and think of how sad it is that they have nothing and I have riches and Queen Elizabeth's ear. How strange it seems to be walking among the common people now. I want to announce to them as I pass that I tell stories to the Queen. Isn't that wonderful! Aren't I very important?

I don't know what is wrong with Alice, but she seems to be sad. She hardly responds to my questions and hasn't smiled at all today. Perhaps Maude has told her off for not working hard enough, as she seems to do to everyone a hundred times a day. Perhaps she is feeling ill again. Or she does not want to be sent on this errand. At least we are together. I will do my best to make it into an interesting walk.

'Look Alice, a goshawk.' I point out a falconer who has trained the bird to land on his outstretched arm. It looks majestic in flight, and I wonder what magic makes it return.

She barely lifts her head. She may be cold. Her nose is pink and sore after her illness.

People here are celebrating and preparing for Twelfth Night too, and I try to cheer her by pointing out the shop displays with their joyful yuletide garlands.

She will have none of it. I'm not even convinced she is listening to me. The hood of her cloak is pulled way over her head. I catch her shoulder, wanting to mimic a group of dancing mummers, and she shakes me off roughly. I'm startled. I believe she is too, for she walks ahead a couple of paces and then retreats to me.

'What is it, Honesty?' She is clearly unhappy.

'Is there something wrong, Alice? Are you unwell again?'

'I am tired. That is all.'

She has been doing some of my duties to cover the time I've spent telling stories and I feel guilty for it.

'We don't have to rush back to the palace, do we? Let's have some fun.'

Alice seems unconvinced but I want to see her smile.

I make her stop to listen to a choir of carollers, then we follow a group of boys carrying a large bowl of spiced ale with roasted apples bobbing in it, the warm scent lacing the air with the merriment of Christmastide.

A procession of brightly dressed men approach. Some of them teeter above us on stilts, their faces gurning with the effort of balancing. Others juggle fire and breathe flames from their mouths. They play the crumhorn pipe and blow cheery tunes on a rackett, enticing us to follow the dancing crowd.

'This way, come on.' I drag Alice after them and even though she tugs in the other direction, I keep pulling her with me. 'Come on, Alice. Come on! I don't want to miss the fun.'

Soon we are gasping for breath and have to stop.

'Where are we, Alice?'

'Southwark. This. Is. Southwark.' She clutches her sides and her words come in sharp bursts between breaths. 'We must leave this place, Honesty.'

She deftly dodges a chamber pot emptied from an upstairs window and gestures between two houses to a path so small I'd hardly noticed it.

'You know this place well?'

'Too well indeed.'

I begin to follow her but stop, disturbed.

'What is that noise?' It is a wailing. A crying. Moaning. Shouting. Terrible and frightening, it draws me closer.

When I find it, arms reach out to beg from behind iron grates.

'It is the Clink,' Alice says. 'And those poor souls are prisoners.'

I feel their pain like a punch to my stomach.

'Come away, Honesty.' Alice puts her arm around my shoulders. 'It does not do to dwell on such things.'

Breaking free of her, I run to leave this place. I keep going until Alice catches me and holds me roughly by the shoulders. I wince, and she lets go of my injured shoulder, but keeps tight hold of the other.

'We must stop running and running, Honesty.' She is stern and brings me to my senses. 'We must go about our business now. Concentrate on our errand and forget this.'

'Forget what?' A man grabs hold of Alice. He snarls at her through stumps of rotten teeth. I rush forward to defend her, grabbing at his neck from behind with my arm, but he manages to shake me off, pushing me away, into a wall, knocking my breath out of me. I slump to the floor, shocked and dizzy.

I see Alice's face crumple and try to haul myself up. I will use my fingernails. Claw at him if I must.

Alice stops me. 'He is my father,' she says, over and over.

'Get away with you.' He swipes at me.

He seizes Alice by the hair and pulls her face too close to his. 'You keep your word and do as you are told. Understand?'

'Yes.' Her voice is strangled.

He strikes her and I flinch as if he has struck me too.

'Running draws attention to you,' he hisses savagely, then lets her go. 'This is a warning, my girl.'

He hacks up phlegm and spits it in my direction then scuffles off. I am aghast.

'Alice, I...'

Wiping her face with the back of her hand as if she can remove the slap, she tucks her hair back in place. 'We must complete our errand, Honesty, and say nothing more about it.'

I follow her, wishing I could find adequate words of comfort. Using the only remedy I can muster, I begin to tell her a story, but she asks me to be quiet, so we walk together in silence.

The package is picked up easily from the tailor and we are heading back to the river when I hear triumphant horns.

'Da-dah!'

People clap at the noise. We approach a round building, covered in emblems flying joyfully in bright colours, reds and yellows, oranges and greens. All the people of London (it seems) are at its gates.

'It is the Globe theatre.' Alice explains. 'The fanfare is to announce a play is about to begin.'

'Oh, how exciting.' I have seen some travelling players in the town square at home and was enthralled. 'Can we hear it?'

Alice looks at me sorrowfully. Her doleful expression makes me feel bad for asking something so silly and I am about to apologise when she pulls herself up tall and nods defiantly.

'Yes, we'll hear the play, Honesty, and no one shall have any say in it.'

A second blast of the horns almost jolts me out of my skin. I shriek with laughter as we join the horde as they stream towards the entrance, untethered from their work for a time. A river of hecklers and revellers, fighting for their place, like the wherries on the Thames.

Alice stops and shows our package to the doorman. 'We have costumes for the players. Made late for this play.'

'We are in a great hurry,' I add, cottoning on immediately. 'If we do not make our delivery before the play commences, there will be some extremely angry actors.'

'And a very vengeful writer,' Alice confirms

solemnly, as if she has great care for the health of the doorman.

'And you know how writers can be,' I add conspiratorially.

'I have seen the way of them,' he says ruefully. 'Why must there be two of you? Do you need to hold hands?' he sneers.

'For shame, I cannot be backstage, with men and boys dressing, without a companion,' Alice replies, sharper than the icicles in the thatch above us.

He takes down the barrier of his arm reluctantly and allows us through. Grinning at each other, we enter the arena.

I have never seen anything like it: round, with the audience seated on three levels and the roof open to the skies. What a wonder of a place. I jostle and point my elbows out, making them as sharp as I can, so I am not knocked to the ground.

'This is the pit,' Alice explains in delight, when we fight our way to the centre where we can look up at the stage and all around us. We dart across it, laughing, wriggling through the smallest of gaps. The crowd swells to fill the space, a beehive swarm of people. I heave and dart and push my way through. I yell at a girl who spills her ale and soaks my hair, but I can barely be heard above the throng. There is every form of stink and filth here. I look up to the 'O' of the white winter sky above and feel freer than a scudding cloud.

Breathless with happiness, I take everything in. The stage has a platform over it where two men play the drums to match my heartbeat. People with money are seated in the covered areas. I'm so overcome I almost knock over a man, stopping too close to his face to apologise. Lice crawl between the creases in his skin, and I back away from him, brushing down my clothes and shuddering.

Alice and I have been separated and she pokes her head between two people's waists to find me. Laughing at how funny she looks, I follow her, managing to barge into a woman who is peeing, beneath her kirtle skirt. The relief on her face gives her away. I burst out laughing again. Fists the colour of ham, she swings for me and I nip in the other direction to avoid her clouts.

Eventually we make it to a spot where we can see everything. I whoop with joy and Alice joins in, so loudly that we make a space around us.

'The view is good from here, Honesty, but

most of the groundlings push to the front without thinking and end up cricking their necks.'

'What are groundlings?'

'Why, us! The lowest of the low and the happiest of the lot.'

I look about me and see that she is right. We, the groundlings, are joyous. Shouting and chanting and drinking and jostling. The others must sit where they can be seen.

I feel a hand at my waist and turn in time to catch a woman trying to snatch my purse.

'I was just admiring it, wasn't I?' She hurries off to find someone else she can 'admire'.

'Hold tight to your belongings, Honesty. There are pickpockets everywhere,' Alice warns me, signalling to an ale seller. We eat and drink noisily, though we can barely hear ourselves for everything is noise here. I laugh out a mouthful of chicken when one of the richest people, who is sitting on the stage so that he can be lauded and applauded, topples off the side into the crowd. I take joyful part in the jeering. It may be cruel, but the poor have lives much crueller than his and we deserve our fun.

I join in with the crescendo of delighted cheers as the players take their places and my heart bursts into bloom. I love it here. I am lost to it. An actor is lowered by a wire onto the stage. Another appears up through it.

'A trapdoor,' Alice explains.

Firecrackers are thrown, causing me, and many others, to scream. They are made with gunpowder but are safe and just trickery, Alice assures me, to calm me down.

I laugh until snot comes out of my nose. Later I hold my chest in sympathy for the pain of forbidden love. Raging with anger, I yell to warn the innocent of his attacker and tears drip from my jaw as he dies, blood bursting from the dagger wound in his chest.

'It's red material.'

'I know.' And yet the death is true to me. This is everything I ever knew that stories could be. The words curl and romp, frolic and gambol, trip from the actor's tongues and enchant us all. Were it not for the pip of a boy who squeaks the young girl's parts, it would be perfection. When the company bows, I cry for more until I am hoarse.

## CHAPTER EIGHT
# ALICE

We stay too late. London is darkening fast. The wind cuts hauntingly down the river. Boats sway, their lanterns glittering on the choppy water. I have known this part of Southwark for years but the fog from the Thames is sly some nights and slinks into chimneys and corners, hiding robbers and turning coaches into monsters.

Honesty chatters away as we stumble down the slimy cobbles to get our boat.

'You tell me the story of the play as if I were not there,' I remark. I'm enjoying her enthusiastic retelling, she even makes some parts better, but I am concerned that we are so late.

Maude will be furious if she catches us.

'This river is the biggest I have ever seen.' Honesty raises her voice to be heard above the slurp of the swallowing waves, once we are aboard and seated. 'It drinks at the land like an angry beast.'

She is right. The river seems to swell larger daily and has taken many lives. Our boat rocks Honesty into a happy silence at last.

Night traffic is less busy than the day but still plentiful. I love this river, despite its stench and violence. I have known it all my life and I admire its power. It cannot be tamed by man.

It takes a long time to get to Greenwich. And the closer we get, the more agitated I become. I'm not supposed to attract any attention. Having managed to stay in the background, and keep myself to myself since I arrived, now I risk being seen as someone who does not obey orders. A troublemaker.

Looking at Honesty, her face lit gently by our lantern and sweet dreams, I feel torn between friendship and blame. If she weren't here, I would not be late.

She gurgles a laugh. It is sudden, as if from nowhere, and I know it is at a memory of the play. It almost wakes her, but she slumbers on. My heart swells. I'm careful not to grow attached to anyone, because of my circumstance, but it is impossible not to feel for this girl, who is so brash and eager and full of pulsing life.

When we eventually get to Greenwich, my fear is so strong I cannot stop the tremor in my fingers. The parcel I have clutched so tightly all the way threatens to fall from my hands.

'Are you so very cold?' Honesty asks me, yawning, mistaking my nerves. 'Here, let me.'

I allow her to take the parcel as we climb up the bank. Although we are bringing it back late, at least we are bringing it back. If I were to drop it into the river now, there would be an even worse price to pay. I imagine the gown floating out into the ocean, like some mythical sea creature. I am catching Honesty's love of make-believe. I take the package back from her. It is precious, and I must stay in command.

We sneak through the gate to the garden. The night watchman knows us and asks no questions, because I give him some good tobacco I bought earlier just for this purpose. Keeping to the darkest paths, we attempt to slip through one of the servants' entrances without being spotted.

'We made it,' Honesty announces too loudly as

we go in through the door. I raise my finger to my lips and she pulls an apologetic face. It is to no avail.

Maude slides from the shadows as though she lives in the wall at night, seeping into it like ink.

'Where have you been?' she screeches in a whisper, which is a talent very few people own.

We freeze. My heart beats fit to burst out through my skeleton. Honesty is also struck dumb. The thunder in Maude's expression; the grey steel of her irises; her malignant delight in having caught us. She sucks the breath from us.

'It's your fault, isn't it?' She points a skeletal finger at Honesty. 'You think that now you are a storyteller, you can do as you please?'

Honesty is deflated. I can see her struggling to think of a reason why we are late, her tongue stuttering. 'I … it … I…'

'You must obey orders if you mean to keep your head. Do you understand me, girl?' Maude's shadow stretches and grows in the candlelight.

'It is my fault.' I will not have this day spoiled by this woman. I will get us out of this. People often mistake my quiet ways for weakness, it has been so all my life, but they underestimate me. I am happiest when quiet, yes, but my character is strong without having to be loud. I hate to see Honesty like this. 'I'm afraid we fell into some trouble, Maude.'

I can feel Honesty's uncertain glances. I hope she will go along with my tale.

'The package was stolen from us.'

Honesty drops her head, that her expression might not be seen.

'We picked it up from the tailor and were hurrying along the south bank towards our ferry when suddenly there was a hue and cry and the clamour of horses behind us.' I want to stop to think but if I leave a pause, Maude will fill it with her disbelief. 'We turned, but too late. The highwayman was upon us.'

Maude folds her arms and tilts her head. She is going to let me make a noose of my words so that I can hang myself. Because I do not speak much, she thinks I cannot sustain my story.

'"Stand and deliver," he demanded. He jumped down from his steed and aimed his musket at us, prepared to shoot. He asked what was in the package. "A gown for the Queen," I told him proudly and then realised my mistake as he scooped us up.'

'He had exceedingly long arms.' Honesty adds.

'And he galloped off with us.'

'All on the same horse?' Maude asks, her shadow growing.

'It was a very big horse indeed.'

As we are talking, Maude's daughter sidles up. She hangs behind her mother, unnoticed, and swaying her skirt as if she is dancing, for children that age are never, ever still.

'We pleaded with him as he rode us out over the moors.'

'Did you?' Maude asks insincerely.

'We did and as we thought all hope was lost…' I falter, as if all hope is indeed lost.

'Alice noticed that he sighed wistfully and realised that he must be in love,' Honesty fills in.

'With you?' Maude scoffs.

'No, with someone who had rejected him,' I return. 'That's why he wanted the gown. For her, you see? We won him over by telling him a poem which would win his true love's heart instead and he set us free.'

'He let you go free and with enough coins to get the boat back here?' Maude asks in disbelief.

I smile and act the innocent. This is a game now. 'In faith. As you know, true love is the only treasure worth having, Maude.'

'If you listen to the town crier tomorrow,' Honesty says, 'he will surely be telling news of a wicked highwayman sighted in Southwark, for all to hear and beware.'

Maude sniffs and is about to punish us when her daughter steps out from behind her. 'What was the poem, please?'

Maude, to Honesty's obvious surprise, takes the girl by the hand. 'You should be sleeping, Nell.' She kisses the girl's forehead. Then kisses Janet the doll's too when it is held up to her. 'It was an ode of love and kindness, and the highwayman took it to the lady he most admired in the world. On hearing it spoken gently, she gave her heart to him immediately.'

'And what happened then?' the girl presses.

'Now he is no longer a highwayman but a good and honest man with a good and honest wife and they lived happily together ever afterward.'

'Did they keep the horse?'

'They did. It was a fine steed who munched rosy apples straight from the trees and slept soundly at night in the best hay,' Maude assures her as she walks away from us.

'What did they do with all the things the highwayman stole?'

'Well, at first, they didn't know what to do, but his clever wife had an idea, and they gave them all to the poor.'

'Will they get into trouble?' Their voices disappear. Only their shadows stay as they round the corner, then their shadows go to bed too. I breathe for the first time since Maude caught us.

We go swiftly to the Great Hall before Maude's forgiving mood switches. Honesty tries to question me, but I put my finger very strictly to my lips to warn her.

Once we have found a spot to bed down, far away from the fire because we're so late, and dismally cold, Honesty creeps to my pallet. The hall is blanketed in noises: snores and gasses, the all too distant fire and the creak of the high beams. I don't think anyone is listening.

'Alice, you are quite the storyteller yourself,' she chides me jauntily.

'Only to save my neck.' My whispered response sounds irked, and I do not mean it to. 'No pretty trinkets for my story.'

'Hmm.' Honesty considers this and I think she realises how I feel. 'But what use is a storyteller who cannot tell a tale to save her own neck?' She does an impression of her earlier self, all shock and bluster and 'I … I … I…'s.

We laugh then so hard our pallet shakes.

'Thank you, Alice. Maude would have had me walking the streets before dawn if you had not made up such a story. I saw that little girl in the garden.'

'It is her daughter.'

'Ah, so now we have seen her heart.'

'And her weakness.' I smile in the gloom. 'I do not think that Maude means to be so hard. Sometimes it is difficult to be kind when you are unhappy in your own situation.'

My voice wobbles and threatens to break, but I manage to hide it beneath a cough.

'Thank you, Alice. I know this feeling well.'

I do not add that I know it well too.

We lie there for a moment, listening to others sleep and thinking back on the exploits of the day. My eyelids begin to droop.

Honesty turns on her side towards me. 'Alice, I must tell you something, now that I know I can trust you and that you are a true friend.'

I make a sound to show her I'm awake, but I am already somewhere on a path to a dream.

'The reason I am in London…' She falters here

and her pause is so drawn out I am far away by the time she speaks again.

'My father. He wanted me to marry someone.'

I snap awake and turn onto my side to face her.

'Go on,' I whisper.

'It was an old man. A merchant. Selfish and rich.' She chatters her teeth together as if her words taste foul. I find her hand and squeeze it. 'We lived in the bottom floor of his house and worked for him as his servants. His wife was taken from this goodly earth, and he wanted a new one.'

Her expression clouds. 'I was going to have to live with him above my own father.' Her face is ashen white. 'It was arranged for money and because my father wanted people to think more highly of him. I was never given a choice.'

She is wrapped up in her cloak as a blanket. She uses the edge of it to wipe the welling tears. The wool is scratchy, so I offer her my sleeve.

'I heard them bargaining late into the night for me, as if I were cattle at market. I waited for dawn, took some money, and stowed away on a coal boat leaving port for Bristol. I had no idea where I was going or what I was going to do. I may not have had to wed him for years. I don't know. I just knew that I could not let myself be sold.'

'I understand.' My heart aches for her. How unfair this life is.

'It took me weeks to get here. First by boat, then horse, then walking, then one stagecoach after another. I tried to find work along the way, but it was not easy and I travelled on a cart for the last part because my purse was small. That's when I met you. I am no storyteller. I'm a runaway.'

I expect her to weep but she is stoic. Her journey must have been so frightening. Her bravery making it this far amazes me. Tucking my cloak around her, I stroke her hair as she slowly drifts into a sleep. We breathe as one.

I want to holler and yell, but I have to keep all my anger inside. These fathers and their wants for themselves. Why should we always do their bidding, putting ourselves in danger and making ourselves sad?

The mounted heads of deer gaze down on us, their antlers throwing strange, demonic figures across the walls and stoking the dark feelings I hold inside. My fury seethes, a vicious rage growing through the night, keeping me awake. Eventually the others begin to stir and I get up into the cold and leave Honesty there, wrapped snugly in her cloak and mine.

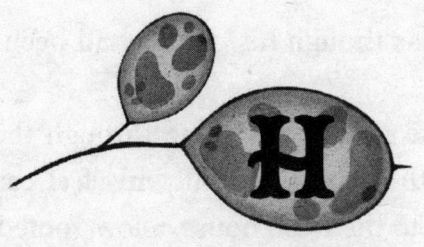

## CHAPTER NINE

# HONESTY

I barely saw Alice yesterday after my confession, as I was in such demand with the ladies-in-waiting. I told stories of the Spice Islands and the Cape of Good Hope and have received sweet treats for my pains. Seeking Alice now, I worry that I have told her too much. What will happen to me if she tells anyone? I had better find her today.

They are skinning a boar as I walk past the kitchens and the thick scent of blood is sticky and sour. They have been working for hours. One of the boys in there is listing everything they've done very loudly as I pass. I feel terrible that they have to work so hard, particularly with Twelfth Night approaching, but when I smile at him, he blushes as though his cheeks had been stung by wasps.

I take my time walking through the gardens despite the cold. Eventually, my feet carry me to the gate to the wash house, a low-roofed building just beyond the palace walls. I'm let through by the laundress and find Alice scrubbing clothes.

'Here,' I say.

She gratefully takes the ale I have brought for her. Washing is thirsty work. The laundress shows me the urine I need to get stains out and then goes back to her post at the gate.

Picking up a stick, I beat at a tub of dirty socks, breeches and other stinking clothes half-heartedly. The sides of the wash house are open to the elements. It is little more than a roof. The river has been channeled to run through it. On a summer's day it might be a nice place to work and admire the gardens. Today it isn't. The wind shrieks through and the cold pinches my cheeks. I'm soon exhausted. This is tiresome. I beat again, feeling the ache of the movement in my arms. Forcing a smile for Alice, I know that I must do my bit to keep my place here and help others. Again, I work. The cold, unsatisfied, nips at my knuckles. The water is needles of ice as it splashes me, and the pile of laundry never seems to lessen. Inside the palace, the ladies-in-waiting are warm. Laughing beside roaring fires. Retelling my stories. My dreaming causes me to slosh water over myself, drenching my skirt, and making me lose my patience. Why should I have to do such a menial task? Yes, the kitchen staff have it worse, but they have solid walls to keep them warm at least. And yes, I know I am a maid who should be grateful for this position, but I cannot help but think that I deserve more. My wit and humour and obvious skill for storytelling should warrant better treatment. I should be a lady. How long will it take?

Alice is now concentrating so hard on beating the washing in her tub that I fear she may break the stick she is hitting it with. A gargantuan pile of linen hangs stiff over a strung line, which shows she has been at work for hours. 'How was your day yesterday?' My tone is weaker than I'd expected. I clear my throat and say it again. 'There is such a lot to do with the feast ahead.'

'Yes, there is.' Alice beats harder, if that is possible. If a team of oarsmen were rowing in time with her, they would race the length of the English sea and be in Cardiff by noon.

Refusing to be cowed down by her banging, I try again. 'You'll break that stick if you aren't careful.'

'It is not a stick.' She stops to wipe her brow with the back of her hand. 'It is a wash bat.'

'You will break that wash bat if you aren't careful.'

She looks up to the heavens in amusement then goes back to work. I go to a sheet which is draped over the line and pull at it a little to make it look as if I too am working. The material has a sheen of sparkling ice already. 'This will freeze here.'

'When they are all done, we will carry them back to the palace and hang them above the fires to dry.'

'The sugar cones have been ground down in the pantry and mixed with almonds to make marzipan.' We share a fascination with sugar. 'I got this for you.'

I hold out the tiniest marchpane apple to her. Perfectly round and green, it could be confused for a real fruit if it were not so small.

Alice takes it and pops it into her mouth. I watch as she savours the sweet taste. It took all my strength not to eat it myself, though I had already eaten three rosewater sugar cubes and seven candied violets.

'There will be so much sweet food at the Twelfth Night party.' I see the happiness brought by the sugar vanish from Alice's face immediately. 'Oh, I know we cannot attend the party but perhaps we could sneak a peek and have a few of the morsels left over for ourselves?'

'The party is not for us.' Alice is immediately glum.

'I know we aren't supposed to be there, but can't we talk about it a little and imagine how glorious it will be?'

Alice does not answer. She takes the sheet she has been washing from the tub and hands me one end. The water dribbles down my wrist and adds to my shivering. I twist the material as she wrings the other end, so the water runs the length of the cobbles into the drains.

This is a terrible chore for someone who has been a storyteller to the Queen. I blow out hard in exasperation. I try to squeeze my energy into wrangling the material and begin a story in my head to counter my growing resentment.

My imagination takes me home. To the day when Gwladyse the spinster put so much soot on her teeth to imitate the Queen that she almost choked to death. How jealous she would be to see me with so much sugar! I shall have black teeth like rich people in no time.

'In my town, one of the women wanted to imitate the Queen so much that she climbed into a chimney-breast with her mouth like this.' I open my mouth at Alice to bare all my teeth. 'She wanted to fill her mouth with soot. Unfortunately, the chimney was very narrow, and she is very not. As far as I know she's still stuck there.'

Alice smiles but her face is still woeful.

I make a decision. 'It isn't fair that we can't be guests at the feast, Alice. I will find a way to get us close enough to see it somehow.'

She doesn't respond.

'Don't you like parties, Alice?'

The sheet drops from her hand so clumsily it is as if she has done it on purpose.

'That will have to be washed again now.' She

states lamely, then puts the whole sheet back into the tub, which is a ridiculous thing to do.

'You could have just put the end into the water.'

She does not reply. She just hits the sheet as if it were a poisonous snake.

'Here I will do it.' I attempt to take the bat but she pushes me away and it catches my outstretched hand. It smarts and she looks as though she will cry. 'What ails you, Alice?'

There is a mark across my palm. I chew at it to take away the sting, then gingerly poke at a bit of washing in a barrel and listen to the *thwack, thwack, thwack* of the wash bat. When Alice has ceased thwacking, I go to her to help with the wringing again.

'Thank you,' she says quietly.

'I'm glad to help you.' We wring the material and share the cold of the task. 'Alice, perhaps now I have confessed something to you, you might also confess something to me? Then we could each carry the burden of the other's secret and lighten our own hearts.'

Knowing my secret gives her power over me that makes me feel uncomfortable. Now that I have seen her father I know that she must have secrets too.

She stops wringing for a long time, staring

at the twisted cloth, stock still. I wait for her to divulge her deepest wrongdoing.

'There is too much work to be done, Honesty.' She tugs the sheet away.

There's something she's avoiding. 'Are you hiding something, Alice?'

Our eyes lock.

Someone calls my name. It is the horse-faced lady I know now as Bridgette and her squirrel. She hasn't spotted me yet and I could easily hide and carry on trying to coax Alice. This moment could seal our friendship. But the draw of being inside, with the ladies-in-waiting laughing at my stories and giving me presents, is too alluring. 'I'm here.' I call, and Alice breaks our stare.

'Oh, there you are, my sweet.' She screws up her nose. 'What is that reek?'

Staring pointedly at Alice, she wafts the smell from her nose. 'This will not do for our finest storyteller. You must leave this place at once and come and tell us some more wonderful tales. The seamstress is here to fit us, and we are all trying out our gowns for the feast. We need some distraction while we wait our turn.'

I feel torn and look to Alice, hoping she might forgive me for leaving her. She is starting on a new sheet and doesn't meet my eye.

Why should I miss out on seeing the gowns the ladies will wear? Why should I be here in this freezing wash house working my fingers to the bone? Why should I be in such misery, when there is a warm fire and laughter and applause waiting for me?

Turning away from Alice, I go with Bridgette and try to ignore the sound of the wash bat's *beat, beat, beat* behind me.

## CHAPTER TEN
# ALICE

I am tired and my legs are heavy. Last night I chose to sleep far away from Honesty. The place I found was damper, colder and far noisier than the space we have used together, and people kept stumbling into me on their way to the latrines, but I am glad to have been away from her. I do not want to lead her into trouble and this morning I have a task which gives me the shivers. I get an uneasy feeling that there is someone following me, but looking over my shoulder I see nothing out of the ordinary. There are servants scurrying this way and that, and they all seem intent on their own work.

A horseman arrives with a message for the

kitchens. His horse brays and whinnies as it is tethered, then munches on oats from the sack. I imagine stealing him and riding out of here. Stopping to stroke his mane, I speak softly into his velvety ear. The star on his muzzle lifts and I see my reflection in his gentle brown eyes. 'You'd get me out of here, wouldn't you, boy?' He answers by sideways munching.

The kitchen master in his counting house raps the pane to make me move along, then goes back to peering at his books. I see no follower in the reflection of his window. And yet I cannot shake off the sense of being pursued. There are plenty of people milling around. Grooms and maids, tradesmen delivering and boys cleaning steaming horse dung from the cobbles.

Perhaps lack of sleep is making me feel this way? Nightmares fill the dark hours, and I know I am foul-tempered and sullen when tired.

I stop, pretending to fasten my poke bag at my waist and turn swiftly, expecting to catch Barnaby at some prank, but he is not there. Something sinister lurks just out of reach and I touch my pomander for luck. Thoughts of my mother swim in, as they always do when I hold it. What would she make of me and what I have become? It does not help to think on it.

I have to go to the tunnels this morning to fetch jams, which are stored there. It is my least favourite part of the palace. The maids talk about seeing strange visions there at night and it is always dark. And yet I must go because I have ill deeds to set in motion.

The cellar is busy with barrels now that Twelfth Night is so close. I am glad of the number of servants, shouting and yammering and working, but the sound falls away as I descend the stone steps. The sputtering candle in my lantern makes little difference against the darkness. Where everything is bustle above, here the noise is dulled by the walls and the damp drinks my footsteps down.

I smile to see two boys heckling and bantering with each other as they pass me, carrying a barrel of salted fish up into the light. Clutching the clothes I am hiding beneath my cloak, I nod to them, their faces ghostly in this eerie light. The boys take their joyful chatter with them, leaving an even heavier silence than before. The cold sneaks to my skin.

I quicken my pace, as much as I can with this feeble lantern.

Here, there are no visitors to see how we work. Here we are kept out of sight. Anything could happen down here.

The groans of the river above mock my misfortune. Water drips, catching me, icier than death. I fear that the tunnels may burst, and the Thames flood in and drown me. Finally, I reach the place where large boxes of summer bunting and items for jousting are stored, and hide the clothes behind them. Sweat salts my upper lip. This is where I was told to leave them.

There is a noise and I wheel around. I see nothing but the dark throat of the tunnel. Rats skitter about and one of them climbs the walls faster than a bolt of lightning. I hurry back.

A little way along, I hear footsteps. Again, I spin to see no one. It must be the echo of my own footfall. I must concentrate on my task.

As I begin my walk again, someone grabs me from behind, their filthy hand across my mouth, their other roughly around my waist to stop me escaping.

'Hold tight to your lantern,' the woman whispers savagely. It's the voice of the woman who gave me these orders. Followed me in the middle of the night as I went to the privy. Held me as she does now so that I could not see her face. Told me which clothes to steal from the laundry. and where I was to hide them in the tunnel. It has been so dangerous, keeping them concealed until this morning. If I had been found to have clothes hidden away, there would have been an investigation and I would have been at risk of torture. I try to bite her hand, but it is clamped too hard to my mouth. I try to fight my way free but she is stronger than me and eventually I stop, rag-limp and waiting.

She moves close to my ear and I am frozen. Petrified.

'You've proved that you can follow orders.' She cackles. 'Now, I have another message for you.' The hiss of words brings with it the rancid stench of decay and something sweeter. Onions. I feel my insides rising and I swallow hard. My candle quivers.

'Your brother says to remember you are to do exactly as you are told. We will always be watching. Understand?'

I nod my head as much as I can against her grip.

'Good girl.'

She shoves me roughly, and I and my lantern clatter to the floor. I put my hands out to break my fall. The pain stabbing my wrists as I land. Her footsteps retreat fast but the sweet stench she leaves behind lingers.

Miraculously, my lantern remains lit. Rigid with fear, I reach for it and shuffle to where I can press my back to the wall. I sit there, on this rough floor, unable to do anything, trying not to puke. Has she definitely gone? Whoever she is, she must work here somewhere. There are so many more maids in the palace for Christmastide and Twelfth Night. It could be any of them. A tear trickles down my cheek and I brush it away. Weeping will not help me. It has never helped me before.

Escape from my brother's orders is impossible. He can get to me everywhere. No dramatic ride to freedom for me. I must do as he says or be killed. He has made that clear enough.

Fetching the jams, I climb the stone steps two, sometimes three at a time. The sky is leaden as I walk through the garden. My fingers burn with the cold, and I can do nothing to warm them.

Taking the jam to the kitchens, I know that I must keep my head down and stay unnoticed.

The strings of a lyre are being plucked somewhere above and are joined by a cheery refrain from the keys of a virginal. The music taunts me from the window, trinkling laughter floats behind. Oh, to be part of such merriment.

I imagine Honesty is the cause of this happy gathering. I picture her there, being given lessons in how to play instruments by the ladies-in-waiting. Perhaps she will play for the Queen one day. Or even alongside her on a spinet, one striking the high keys and one the low. Although the Queen does not make friends, and Honesty has never once claimed to have practised any instrument, these thoughts will not stop jabbing away. Will there be no peace for me?

To make matters even worse, I am to be at the beck and call of the kitchens today for they need help.

I deliver the jams and return my lantern and am shown to my next task. The towers of plates are more than I have ever seen. All to be polished, and quickly. The Queen has these feasts often, but this one is to be even greater than usual.

'Alice, you seem shaken.' Sybil has been with the Queen as long as I and, though we've never been friends, I think that perhaps in better circumstances we could have been, for she is often around and interested in what I am doing.

'I am just weary.'

'I think perhaps you are *weary* because you are taking on the work of others,' she needles, and at once everyone stops working and looks for my reaction. Tired as I am, I do not rise to it.

'Let's get on or they'll have our guts for garters,' I say, hoping this will answer their constant thirst for arguments and brawls.

'It seems unfair to me,' Verity joins in. 'To ask of us that we do an extra share of work while others preen and pose like peacocks.'

Katherine sneezes loudly all over one of the plates. 'The strong scent of favouritism got up my nose.'

'Bless you,' we all say to ward off the devil.

'My sneeze has conjured us bad luck.'

The girls all look behind me and glancing over my shoulder, I see Honesty appearing, radiant with joy, her cheeks pink with the tell-tale signs of a warm fireside. It ignites something within me as bright as a firework.

She comes to stand next to me and sheepishly takes up a cloth. 'What do we have to do here? Is all this to be polished?'

I nod and try to force my anger into the pewter plate I am working on.

Honesty polishes one, then becomes distracted by her own reflection in it. 'I think I shall ask the ladies for a jewelled headpiece for my hair when I next tell them a story,' she muses to herself. 'Perhaps a pearl and gold one would look beautiful. Or an opal and silver.'

I give her no response but she doesn't need one.

'If only my hair were not such a dingy brown. I should lighten it to make it red like the Queen's. I think it would suit me well.'

I steadfastly ignore her.

'Or a wig perhaps. I think the Queen should like it if I were to imitate her exactly.'

I'm so startled by her high opinion of herself that I accidentally drop a plate and the other girls all gleam with excitement. I pick it up and rub at it roughly.

'What do you say, Alice?' she asks. So she remembers that I exist! Her attention is still on her metal face, pouting, stretching her neck and patting her hair.

The furious fire takes over me. 'I say, why should I have to do your share while you prance about like a fool, thinking yourself above the rest of us and complaining when you actually have to do some work?'

I throw the plate down hard on purpose this time. It makes a startlingly loud clattering sound as it strikes the tiles and I hear it circle and circle its metallic shriek as I leave. Honesty hurries behind me.

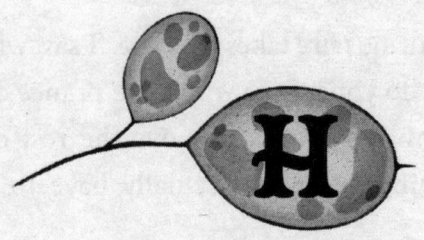

**CHAPTER ELEVEN**

# Honesty

I curtsey to the ripple of reaction. It is so slight even the caged songbird doesn't ruffle its feathers.

'Shall I tell you another? It is more wondrous than the last.' I can hear desperation in my voice. Two of the ladies-in-waiting hide whispers behind their fans. Another glances at me as though I were a particularly nasty boil. Agnes hardly raises her head from her embroidery, and I am certain I hear a muffled snore.

Bridgette stares at me pointedly, as does the squirrel Puck, his eyes beady and bright. 'Aye, tell us a tale, but make it a good one this time.'

There is a smattering of laughter and a few overly dramatic yawns. Agnes, roused by the noise, catches her sampler as it begins to slip down her skirts.

I try to laugh off Bridgette's comment. The heat from the fire makes the small of my back sweat, and embarrassment tightens my throat.

'I will.' Forcing myself to smile, I sift through any stories in my head. They are unreachable clouds, blowing one after another out of my ears. I can only remember snippets and scraps; beginnings and ends, but no middles, or only the main part of the story with no beginning or end.

Perhaps I can string some odd pieces together. Thread them like beads on a necklace until they make a whole.

Wiping my palms on my skirt, I try this. I pace the floor like someone about to tell the greatest story the world has ever heard, while ideas scatter inside me. With one thought comes another but the first disappears as soon as a second arrives, dribbling from my brain like water from a bucket with a leak. I stall for time but they are losing interest. They start to murmur of the jester and his jingling bells and childish japes. If they decide he is more entertaining than me, all the plans I have to be a lady-in-waiting myself will turn to ash.

In desperation I grab for an old favourite.

'I give you the tale of the phoenix and the fire.' I announce.

'That tale is ancient.' Haughty Bridgette recoils in horror at the suggestion of an old story as if I'd slapped her. Puck jolts his chain, fighting for freedom. I know how he feels. 'We want something new, don't we?'

Mutters of agreement.

'Forgive me.' I keep my tone light, as though laughter bubbles in my stomach at my stupidity. 'Something new, it is!'

Bowing with a flourish, I mimic the Queen's fool, and this makes them laugh at least. I have saved myself for a moment.

'I give you the tale of the weaver and the mouse.'

'Heard it.' Bridgette again. I don't know what she has against me but there is something malicious in her tone. She is enjoying my demise. I don't know anything about her, but perhaps her position is as precarious as mine and she is afraid that I will take her place, the horrible, horse-faced nag. I am not usually so nasty about people, even in my thoughts, but she has been longing for my fall from grace since we first met.

There is another yawn and Agnes slumps. A log rolls from the fire and sparks. Barnaby reaches to put it back. His eyes flash mischievously in the firelight. Is he enjoying this debacle too? Why is everyone so against me? My popularity has been hard won and I deserve it, don't I?

'Go and fetch more wood,' Bridgette tells him. 'It is a trifle cold here in both temperature and entertainment.'

He looks at the impressive stack of wood piled up close to the hearth but does as he is told anyway. His place is to do as he is ordered. I'm relieved to see him go. All I need is yet another smirk to put me off my stride.

Thinking back to my hometown, I remember witnessing this sort of shift in a crowd before. Once, when telling a story to the children in the marketplace, there was a sudden wind and catching autumn leaves became more fun than listening to me. You would think these ladies would be better behaved than those shrimp but it seems not. Disinterest is poison to a storyteller, and I am sickening fast. I try a new tactic I learned when making excuses to my father to gain me more time.

'No, I simply cannot tell them that one.' I say, as if musing to myself. 'It is too fearful. I am afraid that they will faint.'

Their ears prick up at this. An audience wants nothing more than a yarn that is not good for them. Only Bridgette retains her haughty expression. One day I will make up a story about a woman who accidentally sniffs up a town with her extraordinarily large nostrils. For now, I will tell the tale of a murderous highwayman.

'One stormy night, as the rain lashed down and owls hunted for shelter in the woods, there was an eclipse.' There is an intake of breath here. Everyone fears an eclipse, an evil omen. I smile inside as they begin to take note. 'A lonely carriage, with a lonely woman inside, galloped across the moor.' They lean towards me. I have them. Such is the power of a story.

'Wolves howled.' I howl loudly and so convincingly that even I shiver at it. 'And the trees hid terrible things.'

Embroidery is now rested on knees and needles dangle by their threads, forgotten. Nostrils, once flared in scorn, are now at rest.

'The wind was mean that night. Keen and cold and filled with spite.'

An audience of motionless listeners hangs on every word.

'The highwayman hid in the hawthorn, ready to make his robbery.' I press my fingers to my lips as if I am afraid to let the words out. 'The carriage, not knowing that the highwayman lay in wait, raced on regardless. Into the trap...'

'Oh, is this the story where the highwayman is trampled beneath the hooves of the horse again? You have already told it, with some very small changes, and we are not so easily fooled as you might think.' Horrible Bridgette. Of course, she would recognise a story with a horse. I glower. 'How many times must we suffer this?'

There is a murmur of agreement from the other ladies, none of them wanting to appear stupid by not recognising it.

'Really, is this all you have, Truly, or whatever your name is? Perhaps we should call for the old fool after all, for this new fool grows wearisome. I long for a tale well told.'

I feel my face flame. She knows my name well enough. And to call me a fool? How dare she? She is one of those people who has to be nasty just to make herself feel good.

I am flummoxed because it is the tale she speaks of, and I have nothing else. I feel like that trampled highwayman myself. I cast about me in desperation and feel my glorious future run away from me, ashamed.

It is at this moment that Barnaby returns, loaded up with logs for the fire.

'No. It is not that story.' I have a chance – tiny, but I grab at it. 'It is the story of the stupid servant boy.'

'Wolves howled,' I repeat, stalling for time again. 'But the boy, a woodcutter's son, found he had run out of wood.'

They simmer with laughter at this. I indicate that I am using Barnaby as the 'stupid boy' in my story.

'Yes, a woodcutter's son should have wood at his fireside, but being so very stupid, he had to brave the dangerous night to gather some,' I say as he walks across the room, not noticing me until one of the men at the fire nods in my direction.

'The carriage came towards him, its stallion thundering through the darkness,' I say, not caring how Barnaby feels, just saving my own skin. 'And because the *stupid* servant boy was whistling a tune, he did not hear it approaching.'

As Barnaby drops the logs onto the pile, I say,

'It was too late: the *stupid* servant boy turned as the carriage was upon him, dropping his wood, and was trampled to death by hooves.'

They laugh and I cannot help but persist. '"I die a stupid servant boy, a woodcutter's son. If only I had thought to get some wood by daylight. Not waited for an eclipse. How stupid of me," the servant boy said. "Perhaps I am an idiot after all," were his very last words upon this earth.'

They point at Barnaby and bend over double with laughter. It is a terrible story, one of the worst I've ever told, but they love cruelty above boredom and eke the moment on.

'The stupid servant boy!' Bridgette calls out, pointing at Barnaby, forgetting to bully me for the chance to bully him. Barnaby's face is redder than blood. I have felt that shame on my own skin and I feel it again now. My blush is not caused by the pop and hiss of the fire. I pull an apologetic face, but he remains impassive. I will make up for it later, if I can. I turn from him as he leaves.

The ladies are pleased for now but how long will this last? They waft me away without praise or payment and all I have to show for my pains is an acid taste in my mouth.

'Perhaps our storyteller has life in her yet?' one laughs.

'Perhaps not,' Bridgette says to Puck, tickling him under the chin.

I hear their scornful laughter as I rush away to find a quiet alcove where I can hide. There, in the shadows, I give in to the weeping which threatened to ruin me. I play the scene out again and again. How dull their reactions were when they saw me. How they have not paid me in treats or coins this time. How close I came to losing my position. What would I be then? A common maid. I cannot let that happen. Thanks be to Barnaby, though I bet he is giving no thanks of his own.

I should beg his forgiveness. But my story could have been of any boy, couldn't it? There are plenty of boys who would fit my description. If he accuses me of making a dizzard of him, I shall deny it. He just happened to be there at the time I thought of the story.

I know this is not true, but what could I do? The ladies must think I am funny and interesting if I am to stay their pet.

Fear of what they will say is taking the stories from me. I am afraid of putting a foot wrong, of offending, or perhaps worst of all, being found to be a bore. I need more outrageous, preposterous or frightening tales to tell.

What shall I do? I am surrounded by the most wondrous things, but they are as temporary as the seasons if I cannot maintain my place. Hidden here in this corner, as the work of the palace continues around me and the day moves into night, I feel absolutely lost.

## CHAPTER TWELVE
# ALICE

I see Honesty coming and ignore her. There are many ruffs to be starched and ironed.

I picture how she will see me. Remembering my reflection in the glass this morning, I know she will notice my hollow eyes, the shadows beneath them. My appearance will make her feel guilty for abandoning me to this work. I'm glad.

My chapped fingers work at the starched frills, pinching pieces together and sliding the poking iron into place to make the curls stiff, one after another after another. Without words, Honesty joins me in the task.

Her hands are soft and glossy, perhaps rubbed with rose and orange-flower oil. Her nails are buffed and shining. The very opposite of mine. If she has hoped for a warm welcome, I'll not give it her.

'Alice.' Her speech is hesitant and her work with the ruffs poor. I glower as she adds one, badly finished, to my pile.

'Alice, how are you today?'

'Ouch.' I burn myself with the poking iron and suck my finger hard. This work is hot and painful. I move her shoddy work aside and press mine down afresh with my palm.

'I'm sorry. I am trying my best.' Honesty says, which is true, but it infuriates me.

'Then your best is not enough. Perhaps if you were to work as much as the other maids here you would be more effective.'

She stiffens and again I am pleased. Biting the inside of my lower lip to prevent myself from talking, I treat the ruffs even more roughly despite the ache in my hands and my burning finger.

Honesty fumbles to refold hers and I bite back an urge to throw them at her.

'I'm sorry, Alice. I will work late into the night to make up for what I haven't done.'

I bristle at that. I raise my shoulders tightly in the effort to keep my fury in.

Honesty tries poking the iron into them more rapidly. Messily. Two of them fall from the table.

A sound of outrage comes from me that I do not recognise. More like a hunted fox than a girl.

'Please, Alice. Nothing is as it seems.'

I seethe but say nothing. I can hear others approaching and I think of my brother and what he will do to me if I am disobedient. I must behave or else all is lost.

'Here she is. Favourite of the Queen.'

'Got any riches to share with us m'lady?' they taunt her.

'Surely you need a posy of flowers beneath your nose to be close to the likes of us.'

'Or perhaps a plague mask,' taunts Sybil, making the shape of the beak on the masks worn by physicians, and croaking like a raven. Her friend thumps her arm hard because no one jokes about the plague.

This sort of teasing would usually make them screech with laughter, but there is venom in it now. I suppose, like me, they are exhausted and don't see why she should have everything when we have none. Honesty tries to go along with their mocking, but it makes the situation worse. Apart from the clothes they stand up in, the mocking is all they own. They are good at it.

'What's this?' One of them makes a swipe at Honesty's waist and takes a handkerchief from her. 'Oh, aren't we grand?'

Honesty snatches for it but they flap it just out of reach.

'I suppose she uses it to mop at her tears of diamonds.'

'Or the emeralds from her nose.'

One of them spits into the handkerchief. This has gone too far now. 'Take it,' she says, thrusting it at Honesty. 'Go on.'

'Leave her.' Stepping between them, I challenge the girl. I am encouraged when her friend takes a step back.

'Ooh, Alice has woken up,' the one with the handkerchief jeers. 'Wouldn't say boo to a goose and now she's making demands.'

I don't know what to say, so I just stand my ground. I try to broaden my shoulders to appear more menacing.

'It's the quiet ones you have to watch.' The other girl takes another step away. 'I always thought there was something about her. She's too quiet. Hiding something.'

I feel the air rush from me. If she has noticed me and thought me odd, then others must have too. They turn their scorn on me now. Such is the way of wars.

'Perhaps Alice is ravaged by madness. That's what she's hiding with her quietness.' The handkerchief-carrier laughs. 'Ready for Bedlam with her unsound mind.'

'I expect she needs to be locked away for her own safety.' Sybil pretends to be me being haunted by visions and walking into a wall. She plays her part very convincingly.

Honesty takes a step towards her and she hoots, backing away. 'Or for ours.'

'Run away!' Scattering ruffs, they hare off, leaving all the work I've done ruined.

'*Diolch*. I mean, thank you.' Honesty helps me to pick the ruffs up from the floor. 'No one will ever know,' she says, shaking off the worst of the dirt. She's right.

We work together in silence for a while, the noises of winter spilling in from the window. Birds calling into the bare, empty, white sky.

People dashing past to escape the worst of the cold. The wind claiming its freezing hold on every turret and spire. A bell knells and the sound rings frostily in the clear, bright, listening air.

Deciding to forgive Honesty, my curiosity winning, I ask, 'What was that word you said before?'

She looks at me in puzzlement.

'Dock or something like that.'

'Oh, *Diolch*. It means "thank you" in Welsh.'

'It's a funny-sounding word. *Diolch*.' I try to make it and sound like a swan when you get too close to its nest.

Honesty laughs. 'I think we should speak in English.'

'The Queen herself speaks Welsh and one of her former ladies-in-waiting.'

'She does?' Honesty is surprised.

If she is as close to the Queen as I thought, then she would surely have known this? I feel suddenly suspicious of everything she has told me. Could she be the one sent here to spy on me?

'If you are Welsh, as you say you are, how do you speak such good English?'

'I *am* Welsh,' she replies, prodding at another

ruff that disobediently refuses to behave. 'Where I come from many people can speak English.'

I am not sure whether to trust her. 'What is it like there? Your town?'

'It is so close to the sea the tide practically laps at the door. Tall ships bring things from all around the world and in winter the storms batter the land so violently that sometimes cliffs tumble, and spume flies through the air leaving everything awash with salt. In summer, the air drifts in fresh across the water, bringing the promise of foreign lands, and rippling the bay. It is all I had known before here. My mother, being from Carmarthen, a town some thirty miles away, spoke fluent Welsh from birth and my father is English. I learned to speak both languages, but my heart is Welsh even when my tongue is not.'

'Because of your mother?'

'Yes. And because when I had sisters, we told tales in Welsh. Ancient tales from long before you and I were alive. Tales of drowned cities and knights in battle. Of men who travelled on a salmon's back and of other worlds beyond ours.'

Checking that no one is eavesdropping, she whispers, 'Of women who are strong and magical.

Women who could charm objects to make men invisible. Girls who could converse with starlings and went hunting alone. Some of the women in these stories even chose husbands for themselves.'

Shocked, I imagine this world where women and girls can have power over their own lives. I work hard as I listen, though I could easily fly away with her words from this world of work. There is too much to be done to give in to it. 'It sounds truly wonderful. Sharing those stories with your family that way.'

'It was.'

'Your sisters? Are they...?' I cannot finish my question.

She shakes her head.

I am sad at how many people are taken too young from this earth.

'I hope one day I will see other places and speak other languages too,' I say. Thinking of Honesty's town by the sea, I cannot resist learning more. 'What is the word for "sea" in Welsh?'

'*Môr.*'

Puzzled, I try it out anyway. It is a word I know of course but not in the same way. 'One day I shall cross the *môr* and see new lands.'

'Yes, you shall, and I shall journey with you.'

'Thank you for teaching me the word,' I whisper, then realise my mistake. '*Diolch.*'

We work for a while, burning our fingers and grimacing. All that time, I roll the globe of the world around and around inside my head like a ball, imagining my freedom. Honesty is quiet for a change. We are happy here, together.

'Alice, if you could have any gift for Twelfth Night, what would it be?'

'Ooh, only one?'

Honesty nods.

'It is a good question.' The ruffs are almost done, and I put the poking iron down, flexing my fingers. 'A gown with pockets in it.'

'Pockets?'

'Yes. A place to keep your things and warm your hands.'

'It would truly be a wondrous thing,' Honesty agrees, satisfied.

'You?'

'I should like to be able to read and write.'

'As should I. Then we could each carry a book of Welsh words. And we could keep it in our gown pockets.'

The ruffs done, we rest a while, pretending to still be at work, though we needn't bother. Even in a palace with so many hundreds of people, it seems you can find space when there are dull things to be done.

'Just one more Welsh word,' I ask of her. It is such fun to learn new things and to have a language that only Honesty, the Queen and I can share.

'*Os gwelwch yn dda.*'

Frothy giggles burst out of me. 'You are teasing me.'

'In faith, I am not.'

'Surely, that cannot mean something.'

'It means "please".'

I scan her face. There isn't even the hint of jest in it.

'Truly?'

'Truly.'

I try the words out behind a ruff. '*Os gweloooch un thar.*' I have several goes before I get close.

'That's it.'

'It's a very long way of saying please.'

She laughs and we sit comfortably like old maids, our hands at rest in our laps, as if we haven't a care in the world.

'Don't let the other girls worry you, Honesty. They are jealous of your favour with the Queen and the ladies.'

'Not everything is as it seems.' Her shoulders slump. 'The ladies grow tired of me and my well of stories runs dry.'

'Why do you not tell them the stories you learned as a child.' I hesitate. 'With your mother?'

But I understand those stories are only for very special ears.

She proceeds to tell me of how she used Barnaby for a story. I am shocked and worry that she will get her comeuppance. Barnaby can be a vicious little weasel. I've seen him put brass pins in people's clothes and stones in their shoes when he feels wronged by them.

For a moment I weigh up the scales of justice. Honesty has ignored me and lets me do all her work. She has chosen treats and favour over duty and left me to rot.

On the other hand, she has shared her presents with me, and I have no real friends here apart from her. Also, it pains me in my stomach to see her so unhappy. Just because I live in sorrow most of the time, why should she?

'I will help you, Honesty.' Of course, I will. It's the most obvious thing in the world to want her to be happy. 'But you must never say these stories came from me.'

'In truth, I will never. I swear it on this crown,' she announces, putting a ruff on her head.

As we go to get our supper, I tell her all I can. The tale of the misericord's wooden face that came to life and sang, which my mother told me when I was knee high. The tale of the harp that played itself for gold that her mother told her before I was even born. The tale of the plough and the pauper that my brother made up for me.

As we take our supper, I relate a tale about a pirate and a firebird, with the lesson that to be away from land with a firebird on board is a very bad choice indeed. These are stories I have known for so long; sharing them that they can be told again feels good. I know that Honesty will make them wondrous.

As we lay on our pallets, I whisper more, though the constant speaking makes my lips sore.

Finally, just as Honesty starts snoring, quick and cheery, I am done. She sleeps deeply while I toss and turn, unnerved by the dark night and an owl screeching as it crosses the moon.

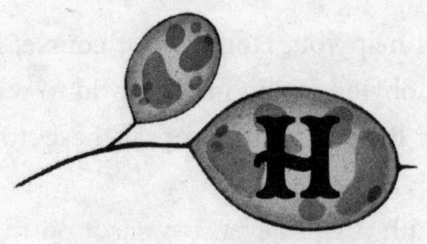

## CHAPTER THIRTEEN
# HONESTY

I wake jubilant and excited. Songs and thoughts of gold have played through my mind all night and I am positively bursting with stories so desperate to be told that the tightest laces and the flattest stomacher could not keep them in. I can hardly wait for the ladies to call upon me.

Turning to Alice to thank her, I see that she has already gone, while darkness still hangs heavy in the room. I wonder where she has crept away to so early? Is she hiding something? I will thank her later, though these stories have become mine now, as I have changed them and rewritten them in my imagination.

My clothes are warm from sleep, and I am

reluctant to get up, but there is little choice as others are already going about their duties and they will not make the effort to step over me for long.

Today is the coldest yet. Rubbing the ice away from inside one of the latticed panes, I peer out. The ground is white with frost and shines where the torchlight catches it. The river holds ghostly mists to its surface and the shape of boats are whispery grey and almost unreal.

Going to the serving hatch, I see Alice already there. She smiles at me, and I return it. We are exhausted, but we are together. She is such a good person to have forgiven me for my good fortune when all she had was work. We scoff down our bread and cheese and gulp our ale. Everyone is always in a rush but even more so now there are extra servants to feed and water.

'Honesty. Alice. With me.' We follow Maude at a pace, weaving this way and that between carts filled with food, casks of aromatic wine, ornate jugs and near toppling towers of plates. To my relief, we don't go towards the wash house. We go past the fountain and climb some steps. Each tread upwards makes me happier. We are going where the rich people are.

In contrast, with each step up, Maude makes herself lower, curtseying to everyone she meets so much we barely manage to walk. She bids us do the same and after curtseying enough to make my knees almost graze the floor, we are pulled into an empty corner.

'You are to be on your best behaviour today,' Maude orders, pinching at our arms to get our full attention. 'They need extra assistance with the gowns for the feast and I have told them, Alice, of your upbringing and knowledge of clothes. Honesty, Alice tells me that you have experience with sewing?'

I nod eagerly. It's not the truth exactly. I've darned a stocking once. I smile at Alice. She has done this so that we can be together for the day.

Creases appear on Maude's face. 'I do not believe you, but be a help to Alice, not a hindrance. I know you have become a friend to the ladies-in-waiting with your story spinning, but life can turn on a ha'penny, my girl. Don't you forget that.'

I assure her that I won't as we set off again, curtseying through this labyrinth of passages.

Unfortunately, we find Barnaby along the way. He sly-eyes me with contempt and I pretend not to notice. It's very awkward and I am glad that Maude has forbidden us from speaking. I have nothing to say to him and fear he has too much to say to me.

'Here.' Maude knocks first, then, getting no response, turns the iron handle to open the door.

In spite of my misery and guilt, I am delighted to see where we are. 'This is where the ladies-in-waiting dress,' Maude announces, sniffing her disapproval.

I cross my fingers, hoping I will be left in this sea of soft fabrics, perhaps alone with Alice so that we can share time together surrounded by beauty for a change rather than by endless work. Oh, how wonderful.

We are ushered in. Barnaby stands at the door while Maude shows us to the various tools we can use to help beautify the ladies. Tweezers to pluck at their hairlines, belladonna for their pupils. Scoops for removing earwax and bodkins for sewing. When she turns and finds he has stepped just inside the room, she scolds him out.

I'm glad to be here, peaceful and surrounded by gorgeous garments, with Alice.

It doesn't last. Almost as soon as Maude is

gone, the ladies-in-waiting arrive, a babble of excitement and expectation, begging us to help them look more beautiful in a hundred different ways.

We are called on to hook a bodice, fasten a farthingale – the hoops of its skirt making the lady appear like a huge church bell – tie the ribbon of a necklace, help secure a wig. It is busier than market day with all the calls and demands.

'I want this to bring out the colour of my eyes,' one of them says, pointing to a corset the blue of a song-thrush egg.

'What jewels shall I wear to make me glitter?' Bridgette asks, believing that she already shines brightly enough and wanting everyone to confirm it.

'I prefer bum rolls,' one of them grumbles, swinging the huge hoops hanging around her. 'This great farthingale makes it harder to get close to the lords.'

They all laugh. Each of them is set on marrying well.

'Seed pearls or diamonds?' Agnes asks, holding a black diamond up to dangle in the 'v' of her heart-shaped neckline.

'Both. Or if you don't want the diamond, I will wear it,' one of the younger ladies answers, adorning herself with anything she can grasp.

On and on come the requests and we do our best to satisfy them, though it is a thankless task. I am not much of a seamstress, however hard I try, but I do have some ideas. I can see how a vitreous-green satin girdle will hang well at a waist, or a shot of popinjay silk improve an embroidered bodice.

Alice and I help them primp and preen and fuss and groan, though they have nothing to moan about. Feathers tickle my nose as skirts and egos are puffed. One sobs because her dress is slightly the wrong shade of indigo. Another wails because she cannot fit her foot into the perfect buckled shoe. Alice and I exchange glances. How little these ladies understand of real life. How would they cope if we were to swap roles for a day? How can they ignore how hard we maids work? How do they sleep at night?

Soundly, I think, looking beyond this room to their chamber where some of them lounge and chitter-chat. One of their beds is big enough to fit six and yet they have one between two. How

I would love to sleep on that mattress, beneath canopies of saffron velvet and russet drapes with gold tassels. How soft my dreams would be if they were cushioned by pillows.

I have only once had a go in a proper bed. At the merchant's house, when he was down at the harbour. I took the bowl of blood up to his room as ordered, taking care not to trip on the trick step, put there to foil intruders and girls whose minds aren't on their work. It had caught me before, earning me a thrashing. How clever I felt not to slosh blood over the sides this time.

Once in his room, I put the blood under the bed to attract bed bugs and tightened the ropes with a wrench to support his mattress. The seaweed stuffing made the room smell like the sea. The bed seemed an all too tempting ship to sail upon. Checking through the window, I could still see him at the harbour, my father with him to unload cargo. A new ship had just docked at port.

Just once, I thought, I'd try it and see what it felt like to sleep in such splendour. I did not mean to nap. Even now I tremble at the memory of being caught. How the merchant came and called my father. How my father said that my mouth must have fallen open in my sleep and the devil must have sneaked down my throat and taken over me, and he would have to be whipped out of me.

I'm brought back from the horrible memory by loud clapping. Bridgette has put a tiny purpose-made ruff around Puck's neck. He tries hard to scratch it off, to the amusement of the ladies, and Bridgette unhooks the squirrel's chain from her arm and puts him into a cage until he can learn to behave himself. I understand how he feels.

Perhaps some of these ladies knew about reality once and forgot it as their lives improved, I tell myself, dreaming of one day being a lady who could snivel over the length of a sash as Helen is doing, even though the others all ignore her. I know, though, that these ladies have come from very rich families and were born to be dissatisfied. And yet, however much they cluck and mither and sulk, I still long to be like them.

'Where is my brooch?' Helen asks. The question hides itself amongst the other calls for a while, but it is repeated at a louder, shriller volume until the others stop.

'It is my favourite.' She is in a high state of anxiety. 'It is a basket and each flower is made of a ruby or garnet, one for each year I have spent with the Queen. She gave it to me herself. Where is it?'

We search high and low. The other ladies forget the hunt almost as soon as it begins, but I feel sorry for Helen, who seems genuinely distressed, worried about the Queen's reactions if she should hear of its loss. Alice and I search among the sleeves and the slippers, beneath cabinets with mythical animals cavorting across them and under discarded clothes. I even search in the garderobe, though I know this is ridiculous. If it has fallen there and dropped into the pits below with the rats and waste, she would not want it back. We find nothing.

Eventually, we have to give up, as the ladies tire of their own reflections and let us go, so they can sit about eating sweets, nuts and gingerbread, discussing the lords who will be attending the forthcoming feast. Other people's business is a hobby they all enjoy. Alice and I overhear as much as possible as we tidy away the garments they have left in sorry piles all over the floor, until Bridgette – of course – remembers our existence and dismisses us with a neigh.

We laugh all the way to the kitchen gardens.

Alice does an impression of doddering Agnes. I imagine out loud the thoughts of Bridgette's squirrel: that he lives in fear of being snorted up by her enormous nostrils and that is why he keeps himself on a chain so that if the worst should happen he can be pulled out. Our laughter, for once, spills out of our mouths rich and full and fat, till we are holding our sides, tears pouring down our cheeks.

When we have laughed ourselves dry, Alice goes to get some ale and I wander in the garden a little more. I wonder what it is like here in the summer when the sun is ripe. I bet the scent of lavender will attract butterflies and bees. The hives are kept safe within the palace now for winter, but will they be brought out here to warm in spring? Honey is one of my favourite things of all.

A rumble in my guts takes me indoors. I go to fetch my shawl from my basket, for the cold has stuck to my skin. Alice is just leaving as I arrive but she does not see me. Perhaps she has been fetching her own shawl too. Opening my basket, I am horrified. It cannot be.

There, sparkling like the smallest collection of flames, is the missing brooch. My heart pounds painfully. I look about me in alarm, then cover the basket again.

How can this be? Who has put it here? Why would someone do this to me? I clutch it in my hand so that no-one can see.

I must return it to the ladies' chamber before anyone discovers me with it. Sweat breaks out all over me. If I am caught with it people will think I have stolen it and I will be imprisoned or worse. My thoughts run on as I try to appear normal by walking at a stroll. Every person I pass is a potential arrestor and will see the guilt written across my face.

Who would have done this to me? Bridgette? No she would have nothing to gain. One of the other ladies? Again, I can see no reason. My mind races uncontrollably. There was no one else there. Except…

The answer is too obvious. Alice. Why was she here when she said she was going to fetch ale?

She was so cross with me and then forgave me so easily. She shared those stories and pretended that we were the best of friends. Her jealousy has been building since I have found my fortune and it has taken her over and made her sly. She has pretended to be one thing while she is another. I can think of no other explanation. Oh, what a callous game to play. To pretend to be my friend again so that my guard is dropped. She is not such a good person after all. She, like the sea, has hidden depths and cannot be trusted.

Alice thinks she can get rid of me? I scoff at the thought. *I will join this game of human chess with you, Alice, and you shall see who will come out queen.*

When I get to the ladies' chamber, my breath is high in my throat, fluttering like a trapped moth. They are all in the Great Hall eating. I make up excuses for my presence here in case I should be caught.

'I am concerned as to the whereabouts of the brooch so decided to take up the hunt anew.' *No, I must not draw attention to it.*

'I have forgotten to pick up my shawl.' *Don't be a ninny, you are carrying it.*

'I must fix a whalebone farthingale. I thought I would do it now so that my work tomorrow is less.' *It's weak but it will do.*

Luckily, there is no one here to question me and I roll the brooch into a dusty corner beneath a black, pear-wood cupboard. It could easily have been missed there in our search. Quick as a flash, I am out again.

I make myself known to the other maids as I fetch my ale. I spy Alice going towards the cellars. She waves as if she were my best friend and I wave back and smile. *I know who you are now, Alice, and what you are capable of. I shall be keeping a very close watch on you.*

## CHAPTER FOURTEEN
# ALICE

'I think, Honesty, were I to wear a gown for the party, I should choose this one.' It has the satiny gloss of a shucked oyster-shell. The sleeves, ready to be attached with their laces, are embroidered with carnation-pink flowers.

'The skirt's a blush velvet and so soft to the touch it is like sifting a dusk cloud with your fingers.' Her way with words is catching. I beam.

Honesty is struggling to turn up a hem even though I have shown her how to do it more times than I can count. She pricks her thumb and grits her teeth.

'Which should you choose?'

These dresses bring me so much joy. The delicious

smell of the material and the way they hang. We are deep in the forest of them and every way you look there are rainbows of splendour. Merry-widow yellow, pansy and orange, watchet blue and the pink of eglantine flowers, deep green like the secrets of a well. 'Honesty, I asked which you would choose?'

She takes the thumb she has been sucking from her mouth and whimpers as a bead of blood forms again.

I laugh. 'It cannot hurt that much.'

I pass her a thimble to protect her thumb tip. She will need them on every finger. Her aim and concentration are so poor.

'Perchance, you would choose this, Honesty?' I point at a dress of mustard-seed yellow, like a shy summer butterfly, which catches the light and traps it in its weave.

Honesty glares at the gown as if it is the ugliest thing she has ever seen.

'Or this?' I stand and dance about in my own maid's garb to try to make her laugh. She forces a smile which meets only her mouth, then goes back to her work. Sighing and sitting, I go back to mine. The frivolity I have tried to bring to this chore is lost as we continue without talking.

I take each stitch slowly, as if I can stretch out time, for I have terrible things to do this evening. Running through the plan in my mind, I know I will be in great danger. The thought of it makes my needle shake and I stab myself accidentally. 'Ouch.'

'You see, it does hurt, doesn't it,' Honesty says, with such malice I am momentarily shocked.

I make an effort to keep my tone light and give a little laugh. 'It does.'

'Yet you can laugh in the face of pain. How interesting.'

I wait. She has something to say, that is clear enough.

'What is it, Honesty?'

Wrinkling her nose as if I were a bad smell, she pulls a face of disbelief. She seems to think I should know what is wrong. I don't.

'What has rattled you?'

'Oh, so that's the way of it.'

'I wish you would speak plainly and tell me why you are so upset.'

She laughs a bitter, hollow bark. 'Why should I be rattled? Amongst such honest friends. The river of kindness flows virtuous and clear here. There is no serpent in it.'

'You are talking in riddles, and I cannot make sense of you.'

'There is nothing to make sense of, Alice. We are good friends, aren't we? Good and truthful friends.'

Confused, I agree and she laughs so strangely again. I too am tired and I have more to deal with than she knows. Before my temper catches light, we are interrupted.

A fuss of ladies enter. 'Honesty, I wish to try out my dress. Has it been altered? I want to choose my periwig to accompany it.'

Honesty miraculously transforms, glittering, coming to life, all smiles in their company.

'We'll make sure you look wonderful. Won't we, Alice?' She is glowing.

Maybe I misread her before. I wish I could stay here, trying out gowns with the ladies-in-waiting. Perhaps they would grow to like me too. See that I am an interesting person, worthy of sharing their laughter. Perhaps quieter than Honesty, but I too can tell a story.

I have other plans. I must ensure my brother can get close enough to the Queen to murder her. Oh, how I wish I could walk away from this evil plot but my father and brother will have me killed if I do not help them. And, however badly I am treated by them both, they are all the family I have left.

'I'm afraid I feel a little queasy.' I say it to Honesty, but one of the ladies overhears.

'Go.' She flicks at me with her fingers. 'In haste. I shall not catch sickness and miss the party.'

Hurrying out, I take one last glance back from the doorway. Honesty is surrounded by gloating ninnies and laughter, and she laps it up like a dog at the water bowl.

I go.

Darkness falls quickly in winter and soon we are all working by candlelight. Many will work late into the night, now the feast is upon us. Eventually, I take my pallet to the Great Hall and lie on it in exhaustion. I hear Honesty drag hers up beside me. She mutters my name a couple of times, but I mumble as if I am asleep. Soon enough I hear her loud snores. Usually comforting, tonight they signal it is time. I must begin.

I try to make no noise as I get up, not to wake Honesty. Many bodies lie in various states of sleep around me, but all those still awake are too tired to care where I'm going. If I am questioned, I will say that I need to visit the latrine and if caught beyond the privies, pretend to be sleepwalking.

I walk along the passageway briskly. I see Maude and have to stop, pressing my back to the wall. Thankfully, she doesn't see me. Twelfth Night celebrations are on my side and many of the servants are still at work, so I do not look out of place. Most people won't question me, but Maude would know that I am up to something.

Making sure no one is watching, I go to my things and put on two cloaks, one over the other.

I reach the garden without being stopped. The guards will definitely want to know what I am doing, but I'm ready. The cold stings every inch of me as I approach. I feel my breath hammering in my chest. It will give me away if I don't control myself.

I take a gulp of icy air, feel it burn, concentrate on that to freeze my nerves as I stride towards them.

'Halt. Who goes there?' Their pikes are at the ready. I step quickly into their light so they know me, and don't axe me or stab me, thinking I'm an enemy.

'I have an errand to run for the Twelfth Night celebrations.' I hold my space and think of strong things. Let the cold in my bones affect the cold in my voice. *Arguments will not be brooked*, I say with my tone. I imagine myself made of marble, statuesque and impenetrable. 'I must fetch a bolt of velvet for the Queen's gown or there will be severe consequences.'

Worry crosses their faces. Everyone knows that the Queen is very devoted to her fashions. I'm certain that, were my story true, they would indeed be in deep waters if they prevented me from obtaining anything on the Queen's command.

'Why must you fetch it now?' one of them asks. It is a fair question, but I am well-rehearsed.

'It is newly arrived from Italy. The ship docked tonight at London, and I am to meet a tailor to receive it.'

They are uncertain. I do not blame them. Everyone is suspicious of everyone here. The punishment for getting things wrong is brutal.

'Why is it not being delivered to the palace?' The blade of his pike glitters sharply. The bell tolls the hour and I let my fear show, putting it to good use.

'I am just following my orders and I am to

meet the merchant some ten minutes hence,' I say, wringing my hands.

'I thought you said a tailor?' There is a threat in his question.

'A merchant tailor,' I say, quickly. Have I lost them? 'If I miss him, I shall have to tell the Queen that you stopped me going. I am fearful of what she will do to you.'

I let that thought hang in the chill for a moment.

'She's just a girl,' one mumbles to the other. 'What harm can she be?'

'Go. Be quick about you,' he says gruffly, going back to his ale.

I'm past them, quick as a hare in flight. Once outside the palace grounds, my fear rises. I have to press both of my hands to my mouth to stop it.

Here there are any number of other dangers I might have to face. Yes, I may be just a girl, but the smallest hole can sink a ship. I must hurry, for time is unravelling and there are wicked things to be done.

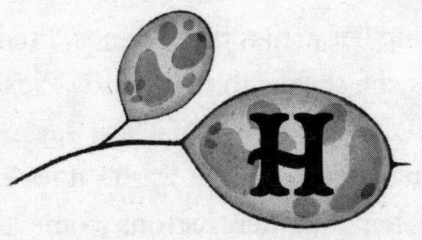

## CHAPTER FIFTEEN
# HONESTY

I am only snoozing lightly, and I see Alice leave. I know she is up to something. I can feel it. Perhaps she is going to steal something else and pin it on me? I continue to snore loudly as she crosses the hall, even though I am wide awake. When she shuts the door behind her, I slip on my shoes.

Luckily for me, Alice has been scared by something and is hiding in the passageway when I go out. Keeping my distance, I sneak along behind her. She fetches her cloak and goes out into the courtyard, which confuses me. This is the wrong way if she is going to the ladies-in-waiting's dressing room to steal something else. I fetch my own cloak and follow.

Stalking her across the grounds, I hide behind a bush as she speaks to the guards, close enough to hear. I am amazed when she says she has a collection to make. I know she does not. They question her, but her reasons come thick and fast. I have seen her lie before and she does it as convincingly as if she were on the stage. Thinking as quickly as I can, I wait until she leaves and then rush up to the guards as if following her.

'I have the payment for her errand. She has forgotten it,' I tell them in alarm. They wave me through as if I am an annoying wasp come to sting them for their ale.

Outside the palace walls, I am suddenly afraid. What if I cannot find Alice in this thick blackness? The river is loud, with the shouts of sailors on the air. Perhaps I will go back and interrogate Alice later? I am at the point of turning when I see her, scuttling along away from the river. Why is she going that way? It is muddy underfoot and difficult to keep her in sight without twisting my ankles in potholes and slipping on mud, but I manage to track her without hurting myself.

She heads up the hill towards Blackheath. I have heard the maids' warnings of robbers and murderers there. It makes no sense to leave the palace in the dead of night, a place with such shelter and warmth, food, drink and safety. But nothing about Alice's actions makes sense to me now.

I'm terrified, and I wish I could turn around. But my curiosity grows greater with every step. I'm determined to discover who the real Alice is. Imagining the moment when I reveal what a deceiver she has been powers me forward. When I catch her up to no good, I will say, 'I knew it, Alice. I knew you were dishonest. You stole the brooch and you tried to frame me for it and now look, I have proof of your terrible deeds.'

These furious thoughts warm me and keep my fear at bay as I track her to some buildings. Torchlights flame against the night and the songs of drunken men fill the air. No. I cannot believe it, even of her! She is entering a tavern!

I am frozen in horror. Why would Alice go in there? Has she been selling her stolen goods? Stashing things with my belongings and then smuggling them out later? Is this how she plans to make her fortune? No highwaymen, cut-throats, or murderers will prevent me from discovering her secret. Nothing, nothing, nothing will stop me.

I pull my shawl up over my head to disguise myself and bend my back to look like a crone, so she won't recognise me, and so I will not be mocked by the men and women drinking and getting up to who knows what in there.

Shuffling forward, I head towards the tavern. The loud guffaws of laughter, the bellows and the pipe music make me shudder. A man comes out of the door and pukes into the gutter. I am reminded of my first day in London with that spewing, seasick soul and think how far I have come. This helps me to brave the last bit and go inside.

The air hangs heavy with smoke. Peering from beneath my shawl I can hardly see through the gloom. There are so many people in here. A man flings a woman in circles until she is giddy and the smoke swirls the pattern of their dance long after they have crashed into a heap.

Men and women smoke clay pipes and silver pipes, long pipes and short pipes. Tobacco litters the tables. Choking, I make my way through the horrible place looking through streaming eyes for Alice. I stay close to the walls so I will not be accosted or swung by the arm myself.

Tucked away in a dark corner, I see her. She is

talking fervently with a man. It does not look as if she is selling him anything, or if she is, he is not happy with his purchase. They seem to be quarrelling from the way Alice flings her hands about. He keeps glancing over his shoulder, and he looks so on edge I wonder if he is being hunted by someone.

She takes off the cloak she is wearing and she has another beneath it. She gives this second cloak to him, then puts hers back on. I do not understand.

He suddenly grabs Alice by the hair, so roughly I almost go to her rescue but, I am ashamed to say, I do not.

He pulls her very close to him and says something into her ear before hurling her away. Alice slams into a stool, holding her head in pain. He picks up his beer again.

'We have a new wench to dance with!' Someone grabs my waist and I am dragged by my shawl, as Alice picks herself up and leaves. I struggle for all I am worth, forcing my fingernails into the man who tries to jig with me. I scratch at him like a cat, drawing blood. He staggers back and I scarper, away from his grip, away from this devil's pit, and out into the Greenwich night.

I find Alice waiting.

'Honesty! What are you doing here?'

'I could ask you the same thing.'

'Quick. This way.' She pulls my arm then we run until the tavern is far enough behind us and we are safe to stop. I have a pain in my side and am panting for breath.

'What are you doing out here?' I am shaking all over with shock and cold and anger. 'Why were you waiting for me, Alice? How did you know I had followed you?'

'I saw you at the tavern.'

'Yet, you did not come to help me?' Scalding rage rushes through me, though I did not go to help her either. 'Why did you go to that forsaken place?'

'I cannot tell you, Honesty.'

'Cannot? Or will not?' I am seething. 'Who was that man you were with?'

It is too dark to make out her expression.

'He is close to my father.'

'Your father?'

I can feel that she is making a motion with her head. 'You must speak plainly, Alice, for I cannot see you well.'

'Yes. I went to meet with him because my father wanted me to give him a cloak I had repaired.'

This rings true. I watched her give him a cloak. 'Why did he attack you?'

'He thought my work was shoddy.'

The rogue. Her needlework is superb. 'Why did you not meet him in the day?'

We walk side by side now, close enough for protection, but not close enough to be friends.

'I met him by night because he ... he is up this way on business.'

'Why, then, did he not meet you at the palace? Is this another lie?'

There is a pause. All I can hear is the ticking of my one heart and the stamping of our four feet.

'It is complicated, Honesty. What do you mean, "another lie"?'

'The brooch.' We are getting closer to the palace. Its bulk is outlined against the night, well-lit and filled with listeners. I must pursue this now while we have this moment of freedom. 'Why would you steal it and plant it in my belongings? Tell me, Alice, are you trying to have me executed?'

'What?' I still cannot see her, but she sounds incredulous. 'What are you talking about?'

I tell her, as if she didn't know, how I found the

brooch and where it now lies, twinkling beneath the cupboard.

'I swear to you, Honesty.' Alice halts and I stop too, for the pain of this moment is too much for me. My throat is tight. 'I know nothing of this. Nothing.'

I almost believe her, but who else would have done it?

'Honesty, I swear to you I did not take the brooch.'

She sounds as if she means it, but I am wary of her now.

'And I would never do you harm.'

I keep my doubts to myself, swallowing hard. 'Let's get back before we are missed.'

The walk is tough and brittle cold. When we get to the palace, we wait for the changing of the guard, as this is when they will be least interested in investigating two maids who have run out on an errand. Alice has a bolt of material with her, which she smuggled out under her skirt, to confirm our story when we are stopped. The weary night-watchmen are as exhausted and ready to sleep as we. They search us briefly then let us through without questions.

We go to our hard beds gratefully. Just as suspicion carries me into slumber, the cockerel crows the dawn, and it is time to get up.

**CHAPTER SIXTEEN**

# ALICE

The day of the Twelfth Night party is upon us. Everyone rushes about their chores. Dread seeps through my soul. This is the evening I have been hoping would never arrive. I find where the laundress keeps the key to the wash-house gate and take it, hiding it under my clothes. There will be no washing this evening, for everything is already done, so nobody will miss it.

In the ladies-in-waiting's dressing room, their clothes are all set out ready. Each will be radiant with their colours and jewels. How I wish I could have a small piece of such delight. To dance and cut a caper carelessly. To flitter like dragonflies. Eating and laughing with friends over the latest scandal at court, discussing who has travelled from where, who has the most attention from the Queen, who is betrothed.

I ensure that my hands are clean before beginning to pat the dresses down, checking them for dust and moths. Pressing the velvets and satins firmly with my palms, luxuriating in the feel of them against my rough skin, is a soothing job and I enjoy it.

To my surprise, there is another dress here. One I have not seen before. It is smaller than the others, but would fit me well, if a little short. It dashes through my mind that I should try it on. There is no one around. I push the thought away. These dresses are not for the likes of me.

Would it hurt though? Just to see how it would fall and feel. Holding it in front of me, I gaze into the looking glass. What would it be like to have just the smallest slice of this other life? I'll slip it on, for the briefest moment, to feel the wonder of something so rich and fine next to my skin.

A couple of maids come in, awkwardly carrying an extra looking glass, banging into the carved wooden door and toppling a bowl of oranges studded with cloves. I know them. They are as thick as thieves, always waiting for their next opportunity to poke fun.

I sweep the dress with my hands, brushing rapidly downwards. 'Just shaking out any possible moths,' I explain.

'Isn't it delicate?'

'It is.' I sweep less harshly, taking in the scent of the cloths. I have loved the perfumes of rich materials since I was a child, when my father used to work with them and teach me about their warp and weft. Happy days, long gone.

The girl with the turned-up nose looks over to her friend, who has a nose as sharp as a knife. 'She's so lucky to have been given it.' They move closer so they can admire it. 'And to go to the party too.'

'I should like to go to the feast.' Sharp-nose is less sharp when she is dreamy. 'And join a galliard.'

Humming a tune, she hops from foot to foot. One bows, the other curtsies, then they do away with any ceremony and prance about foppishly, making each other laugh until they can barely stand. Tempted as I am to join in, I know my place and the care of these garments is important to me.

'Be careful with them.'

The two stop, though their laughter continues

to spiral joyfully into the eaves. Waiting for them to catch their breath, I think how lucky they are to have such a jolly friendship, then wonder how they know so much more about its owner than I.

'Whose dress is it?' I ask. There must be a new lady-in-waiting.

'Why, it is Honesty's dress,' Upturned replies in astonishment. 'Did you not know?'

The other, who is bent over, her hands on her knees to recover, beams up at me. I can feel them knitting gossip thicker and thicker.

'With her being your constant companion, we felt sure you would have been the first to know,' she says through a mouth full of teeth.

My face burns. 'I must fetch something.'

Turning away from their giggles, I run out into the passageway, straight into Honesty.

'Argh! Alice. You nearly knocked me down the stairs.' She holds on to the wall and regains her balance. I cannot speak. 'I have been looking for you.'

'To tell me about your dress?' I sneer.

'Have you seen it? Can you believe they gave me something so exquisite?'

'No, I cannot,' I spit.

'Are you rushing somewhere? I am going to go and gaze at it.'

'I cannot take time to gaze at anything. I am still a maid here who has to do work and doesn't get given beautiful things.' Pushing past her, I descend the stairs two at a time.

Red rage carries me along until I come to a stop outside the Great Hall. Its yuletide glory should bring me great joy, but it flashes so bright against my pain I can barely open my eyes. Gold and silver shines from every surface. Golden candlesticks and ornate jugs on every table, so polished you can see the stained-glass colours of the windows reflected in them. Each space is decorated lavishly with evergreens and garlands, and a kissing bough of mistletoe is hung at one entrance. It is spectacular.

This is where the players will assemble to perform for the Queen. There is where she shall sit. Here the guests will enter to be introduced.

And here they will watch the events unfold in horror.

I shall be glad to be free of this place.

I will not be allowed in tonight. Only men can serve. But I must find somewhere to watch, so I can see my brother do the terrible thing. I cannot even think of it, it is so horrific. My knees shake, and I lean against a table to hold myself up.

A woman passes carrying a tureen of mulled wine which laces the air with sweet-smelling spices. She studies me. Is she the one who is spying on me for my brother? Another walks towards me like a fox closing in on its prey. A third peeks at me from behind a pillar. A fourth...

My head spins. Every woman and girl who passes me could be the one who threatened me in the cellar. Who knows how many spies there are, making sure I do as I am told, ready to attack if I don't.

'Do you need something?' One of the grooms stops and studies my face in concern. 'I can get you some ale if you need it?'

'That's very kind of you. I will be quite well in a moment.'

My head rings with dark and dreadful deeds. I try to stop the panic creeping over my skin. Concentrate on the stags' heads mounted on the wall, their glass eyes dead and dull. They were once free. I can't remember when I last felt free. My brother and father have scuppered any freedom

I might have had since my mother departed this world.

Once I have my wits about me again, I survey the hall, looking for a place to hide. The musicians practise their pavanes and I make a show of being busy checking the laurel wreaths and gilded fruit. As I have been instructed, I unlatch the window, the one directly opposite the tide-clock tower. I wander about, skirting the room and tinkering with decorations, until I find a nook just away from the serving doors. I think I can sneak into the space behind the tapestry here, if I am deft enough. The guests will be too distracted by the party to notice a maid.

I go back to the ladies' dressing room, for I have work to finish, and am met by a caterwauling so shrill it hurts my ears.

'You! You did this!'

Honesty is brimful of anger, her fists pulling at her skirts and her lips snarling.

'Did what?'

Stepping aside, she thrusts her finger at her dress. It has been slashed. There are sharp holes in places and in others it is cut into ribbons.

I stand open-mouthed, unable to speak.

'You are so jealous of me, Alice.' As if possessed by a demon, she pummels her fists against her thighs. 'You've been jealous of me since the first day we met.'

'I...' am agape.

'I am funnier than you. Wittier. Luckier. Fortune has favoured me, Alice, and you cannot take what I have been given. It is my right to have these things.'

This galls me. 'Your right?'

'As a royal storyteller and friend to the Queen.'

'You used my stories.' I am quaking now, upset but also confused and angry. 'I gave them to you.'

'I took your dull, flat, empty stories and I made them gleam. Without me those stories are nothing. A string of humdrum, dull words, putting their hearers into a very sound sleep.'

Her words fizz and sting. I have held those precious stories in my heart. They have saved me in my worst hours. It is too much and all my anger evaporates, the energy wrung out of me by her spite and by how wrong I was to believe in her.

'Your envy will not win, Alice. Do you hear me?'

She moves closer. Afraid she will hit me, I cower back.

'I will get another gown. An even more beautiful one. And while you work, I will be at the feast, eating the finest foods, drinking the best wine, and having a wonderful time without you.'

She pushes past me so roughly I cry out. Without stopping, she storms through the door and is gone.

I feel the weight of her words long after she's left.

I examine the cuts to the dress. This damage was not caused by me, but I can see why someone would want to hurt Honesty. She is hateful. As life carries on outside the room, I am suspended in this moment, the pain as sharp as a thousand pins.

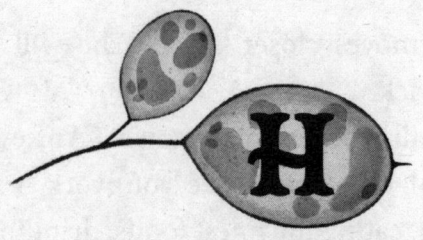

## CHAPTER SEVENTEEN
# HONESTY

Alice is no friend of mine. I have not seen her since I discovered the damage she did to my dress, and I am trying to avoid her, a task made easy by the hundreds of people there are working here now. I knew her behaviour was strange. I knew she was keeping secrets. This is why. She was waiting for her opportunity to ruin things for me. Jealousy is a powerful monster, and it has Alice's green eyes.

Thinking of her startled face, I begin to doubt. Surely, she is not that good an actor? And yet I have seen her innocently get past the doorman at the theatre and the guards at the gate. I thought I could trust her. Having always believed myself to be a good judge of character, I am perplexed.

I step into the courtyard to breathe fresh air. The palace looks so glorious from the outside this evening. Lights glow from every window. Figures pass the diamond panes, carrying and fetching.

I stamp my feet and cup my hands, blowing into them to warm them against January. Tiny flakes of snow fall, glowing in front of candlelit windows, then pinpricking the ground yellow in the window light or glimmering silver elsewhere, before they melt and are gone.

I think of the stories Alice and I could have made to suit this night, with its crystal-cold snowflakes caressing the garden like kisses, and the blazing windows so defiant against the dark.

I think of home. Happy as I am to have escaped a horrible marriage, there are things I miss. I wonder whether it is snowing there too, though it rarely snows by the sea. I wonder if the port will continue to thrive – the modern boats have keels too deep for the harbour. I wonder if my father will survive that and the shame of my running away. I wonder if Twelfth Night will bring the town together in merriment and revels as it used to do.

It is too cold to stand here musing and worrying. Regrets are pointless, and guilt is a worm which eats away your flesh. Wrapping my cloak around me, I head towards the holly bushes. Maude has sent me to fetch some branches. This feast has been a bit much for her and she flails at the slightest thing and presses at her chest about fifty times a day.

Crossing the gardens, I inhale the bitter scent of nutmeg on my fingers and look forward to finishing work and joining the feast. The snowflakes, barely floating dots a moment ago, are already beginning to thicken and I think they will soon fall fast. I am good at predicting the weather from the hours I have spent outdoors, avoiding my father and his consistent foul moods. Recalling his many beatings in all too vivid detail reminds me why I fled.

I am snipping a sprig of holly with some scissors when I see the players arrive. How unfair it is that girls cannot be part of their troupe. Surely I could make a more convincing woman than the boy I saw with his pipsqueak voice and all too frequent tears?

I recognise them! These are some of the players I saw at the Globe. Wait. I halt mid-snip. One of them is the man Alice met at the tavern. The braziers are being lit along the pathway and they illuminate him clearly. I am certain it is him. He glances over his shoulder even now, as though the devil was chasing him, just as he did before. She did not tell me he was an actor. Another lie to add to the many. I am befuddled. Who is Alice? This girl who pretended to be so quiet and truthful?

The guards inspect the players' trunks and then they are permitted to take them across the courtyard to the servants' entrance. The young boy who plays a girl brings up the rear. He drops a glove on the ground in the sparkles of snow but doesn't notice. I take my chance and pick it up.

'Well met by moonlight,' I call, pretending to be pleased to see him. 'You've dropped something.' He looks back uncertainly. Flames from the torches lick his face orange. The others walk on ahead.

'Here,' I say, waving the glove, but not moving towards him.

He checks where the others are heading and hastens back to me.

'Give it me,' he demands with an arrogance that tells me he thinks himself a fine actor and well above a maid.

The hairs on my arms bristle and I grit my teeth and turn it to a smile of sorts. 'I shall. But first you must answer me a question.'

'I must do nothing.'

I stand my ground, holding the glove behind my back.

He looks to see the others, but they are no longer in sight. 'What is it? Be quick.'

It is my turn to act. 'I am a great fan of you players with your wit and skill.' I will say good looks if I have to, but I will not add this lie willingly.

He looks pleased. Flattery is a powerful tool.

'I recognise you, of course, for you played your character with such grace at the Globe. How could I forget?'

Any other person might protest, but not he. He strokes his hair and nods at his own brilliance. 'Why, thank you.'

I want to pop him with the holly.

'I hear that Master Shakespeare only employs the very finest players.' I let this ring in his ears. 'I recognise all but one. Is there a new actor in the company?'

*I am quite the actor myself, aren't I?* I say to this impudent boy with my beaming smile. I should be so good on the stage if only I were allowed.

'Oh, that surly fellow?' He says this curtly, wanting to continue talking about himself. 'I do not know him well. He joined us recently and has yet to make his mark. I have played many roles and had many doting audiences.'

'I am certain of it.' This vain, onion-eyed barnacle.

'Give me the glove. I must go. I have to keep watch over him, for he is a drunkard and took far too much ale last night. He has a few lines, and otherwise bangs a drum, but who knows whether his memory will be able to store the words. I myself can remember whole passages by rote, naturally.'

I am tempted to toss the glove into the holly bush. Instead, I dance it in front of me.

The boy scrutinises me. 'When he was drunk, he was rambling about having a sister here at the palace. It's not you, is it? This is just the sort of thing a sister of his would do.'

My blood rushes hot through my veins.

'He says she does whatever he orders her to, so if it is you, and he forgets his lines, I shall make sure he knows it is your fault for keeping me here.'

The cheeky little rat. I drop the glove on the soaked ground.

'Oops. I'm afraid my fingers are too numb with cold to pick it up.'

He grabs it and runs after the others, leaving

me in the swirling flakes of snow with swirling thoughts to match.

His sister? Of course. Why else would Alice have met with him? Could he be her brother? But why would she lie yet again?

I deliver the holly, pitiful gathering though it is, and I hurry away before I am sent on a further errand.

At the ladies-in-waiting's dressing room, I am welcomed by a hive of activity as the ladies prepare for their own performance.

'Honesty, can you fasten this?' I do so with brittlely cold fingers.

'What do you think of this, Honesty?' One of the ladies, who has hardly bothered to speak with me before, asks advice on the placement of an ornate headpiece for a flamboyant wig. It makes her head look like a big orange, but I smile sweetly and 'ooh'. Let her read my reaction as she will.

They have all chosen their dresses a hundred times over, had them fitted and altered, shed tears at a piece of handcrafted lace that is not quite fine enough, or a jewelled bodice that is not as jewelled as another. And yet they are enjoying the fuss of last-minute changes and improvements. One of them, whose name I forget, is crying *again*.

'You must get ready for the feast yourself, little pet.'

Crestfallen, I stare at my toes. 'My dress. There was an accident.'

'That maid, what is her name?' Bridgette inspects herself proudly in the looking glass. Puck, on a golden chain for the party, pulls at her ruff and she smacks his paw away. 'The one you are always with.'

They must know about Alice ruining it. I stay silent, feeling the dregs of my anger starting to fizzle like gunpowder.

'She fixed it.'

My head snaps up. I have been avoiding Alice today though I know she has been working in the dressing rooms.

'She was supposed to be putting the finishing touches to our dresses.' Bridgette whines horsily. 'And instead, she hid behind there –' she points halfheartedly at a far corner with a screen '– to work on yours. She will have a good, hard slap for her timewasting when I see her.'

I go to the screen and nervously walk behind it.

The dress is even more stunning and shimmering than before. Leaves have been hand cut from various materials and sewn on to cover the holes. Where the cloth was slashed to ribbons, it now flutters with lace like the falling snow outside. Its sheer beauty makes me gape.

'You might want to close your mouth before you put it on, for fear of dribbling over it,' one of the ladies says, as in a whirlwind of fluttering fans and clattering heels, they all go, and I am left to admire Alice's work.

Dressing as speedily as I can without help, glorying in the rich material against my skin, I feel my stomach sink. The dress should make me happy, but there is guilt in every stitch. Happiness comes from within, not without, however glorious the attire.

Dabbing at my eyes and nose with a handkerchief stitched with bluebells and a 'H', I make my way to the Great Hall, trying to be invisible, for though this dress is a thing of beauty, it hides my nastiness within it. My hasty suspicions have made my heart as rotten as a canker blossom. How have I become this person? I search my soul, as I greet the lords and ladies, all of them in high spirits and dressed in their finest.

Catching my reflection in the diamond shapes of the window, I see myself dissected into pieces. Separated bits of me in each tiny pane of glass. Who am I? All these segments of who I thought I was and who I might be. Can I reassemble myself? Perhaps I can choose to make myself different?

Turning, I stand in the doorway to the banquet hall, blinking in the light of a thousand candles. Hundreds of people and yet there's only one I want to see. Perhaps there will be time to go and find Alice before the feast begins?

The Queen has not yet arrived and so there is a chaotic tumble of activity and noise. I am about to turn and go in search of her, when Bridgette catches me by the elbow and escorts me to the other ladies-in-waiting, harrumphing at me for walking in the wrong direction and whinnying with excitement at the party.

I want to enjoy this evening, but something uneasy stirs within me. We are on the brink of something very, very wrong. I cannot put my finger on it, but I feel it creeping in at the edges. Something very bad is going to happen.

## CHAPTER EIGHTEEN
# ALICE

The night of the feast is here and I am hidden. A gap in the rich tapestry gives a chink to view the hall. My heart thuds to the beat of an execution drum. I have made a decision. I am going to stop my brother. Signal to him somehow. End this madness.

I see Honesty enter, surrounded by merrymakers. The dress I have worked so hard to mend is vibrant and ethereal. The leaves seem to be drifting as she walks. I watch as she is hooked by the arm to the ladies-in-waiting, gabbling and batting their eyelashes at potential suitors. The Queen shall soon arrive and though the hall is festooned in golds and greens, the candlelight bewitching and the company jolly, a nightmare will soon be upon us.

Is it too late to stop my brother? I have no way of knowing where he will be before the attack. He may have been hiding at the palace for hours now. He has other help on the inside, that much is certain, though I don't know who the woman is. I should go and search for him. Try everything I can to find him. I am afraid. To watch the Queen's murder. To die myself.

In panic, I try to think of ways to end this nightmare. I could leap from behind the arras and knock a large platter to the floor to distract everyone. I could drag my brother away before he makes his attempt. Convince him to leave, but I have never been strong enough to stop him doing anything. I could rush to the stage and, grabbing a dagger, plunge it into him instead. But no, he is my brother. I could…

A fanfare heralds the Queen's arrival and I press myself back against the stone wall. The hall falls silent, except for the roaring fires. A few hundred people all waiting with bated breath for a glimpse of Gloriana.

I should run from here. I should save myself. It is too late.

The Queen enters. Peeping from behind the

tapestry, I gulp in wonder. I have never seen her look so stunning and fearsome.

She is all jet black and gold: like precious metals come to life. Her gown has the magic of alchemy, bewitching all with its spell.

Stunned into silence, the crowd bows and curtsies. She nods to some of them as she passes and her ladies-in-waiting join and trail behind her, like bees protecting their queen.

Taking her throne, she waves a hand so that the music may begin and then rests her arm on the chair and her chin in her hand, holding her head up. There is something so sad about her. Her melancholy sits on her shoulders. She seems as lost in this great festivity as I am.

I have not eaten and the smell of the meats as they are carried past make my stomach churn. Platters are carried to the tables: whole peacocks baked into pies, their heads protruding from one side of the pastry and the fan of their tails at the other; swans; a cockatrice, a pig's head sewn to the bottom half of a turkey, carried by two men because the platter is so heavy; love apples; peach pies. The strong, heady scent of Malmsey and Claret wines make me dizzy. Such rich foods and drinks sicken me. I am sickened by the people guzzling and gorging. I am sickened by all of it.

Honesty is now seated with the ladies-in-waiting. She glows in the candlelight, and I feel happy she is enjoying this feast, at least. I pray that she will be safe.

'Farewell, Honesty,' I mouth, knowing that she will not hear me. *Do not think too badly of me.*

The feast lasts so long, I begin to think it will never end. Course after course is devoured by the nobles, lords and ladies. So much food is left and wasted. The servants will be looked after well and after that the hounds, then perhaps the poor will get the rest. I hope so. There are too many people starving on the streets, forced to steal or worse to eat.

The musicians play as the lords and ladies take up their lines for an almain. Partners bow and curtsey to each other, then the dance begins. While they press their palms together and spin in small circles, I watch Honesty. As the dancers hold hands and walk and hop in a large circle around the room, I hope she will spot me here, impossible as it is, and save me. The last chord sounds and there is a smattering of applause and rapping of knuckles on tables. I cling to the stone wall behind me as the horns sound again and the entertainment begins.

A player enters and walks slowly to the centre of the room, waiting for the guests to hush. He bows first to the Queen, almost scraping the floor with the tip of his nose, then opens his arms wide to all of us. My heart is in my mouth as he speaks.

'Here, for the delight and delectation of Her Majesty Queen Elizabeth of England and Ireland, we, the Lord Chamberlain's Men, begin our performance of the most wondrous of comedies by Master William Shakespeare.'

At this, Master Shakespeare comes forward, confident, his eyes twinkling. He bows to the Queen, and she smiles for the first time this evening.

'Master Shakespeare.' He is a favourite of hers. 'What tale of merriment do you bring us for Twelfth Night?'

'Ah, Your Majesty, a tale of shipwrecks and mistaken identities, of japes and pranks and misfortune, but most of all, of love.'

The Queen giggles, a rare sight indeed. Some of the ladies flutter their fans for they are easily won over by writers.

'Your Majesty, for your entertainment, joy and amusement, we bring you *Twelfth Night or What You Will*.'

One of the players comes in, playing a drum and a recorder at the same time, then another enters with a flute. A third blasts a cornet rudely, which sets the audience laughing, and then the three start a tune so sweet it pulls the strings of even the hardest heart.

Another player takes centre stage.

'If music be the food of love, play on.'

And so, the story begins. Oh, how I wish I could enjoy it.

It is a tale of a near-drowned woman and a drowned brother, it seems. It holds a mirror to my life, for my brother is lost and I am close to drowning too.

The crowd is restless at first. The play is too serious for such a celebration, and I see some of the guests lean in like wolves, eager to give their critical reviews. No need though, for soon the tale changes tack and we are sailing through seas of laughter. Everyone is laughing but me.

My brother enters blowing a pipe. Even now, I try to think of ways to stop him. He stands back, waiting for the audience to be so in thrall to the story they will not see what is coming.

There is nothing, nothing to be done. I am too afraid. I should have stopped this before now. I want to run, to drag him away, cause a distraction, but my legs fail me. I want to flee and save myself, but I am frozen here in horror.

I watch as he comes a little closer to the Queen. Her protectors shuffle at her sides but do not pay heed to him. Honesty is too close to the Queen. Her face shining with happiness.

Closer still he moves, his mouth a crimson slash, his eyes aflame. Time slows down. The moment stops in the air.

He pulls a pistol from the hidden pocket I have sewn into his cloak and shouts, 'For my father.'

Time speeds too fast as he shoots.

Screams and chaos. Honesty is thrown aside by shock, but not shot. And suddenly I find my feet again, slipping from behind the tapestry and escaping out into the passageway. Servants are chasing past me in all directions. I keep going, past the fountain, snow tumbling around me. Into the wine cellar, nearly empty now the feast is done. Down, down, down into the dark tunnels.

Quiet, but for the echoes of the river. I find the clothes where I hid them. I hold them close and I wait, my breath rasping painfully in the dark. Someone has lit a torch at the tunnel's entrance, but the light does not reach here. I am eaten whole by the darkness.

I play out the events above.

Someone will grab at my brother's cloak, but it will unfasten itself for I have sewn it that way.

He will miss the window I have unlatched for him to escape through. No, I have explained to him which one it is so many times over. The one opposite the tower with the clock that tells the tides.

The guards will catch him. And yet, I know that he is nimble. He has firecrackers in his pockets which he will throw to create confusion with their noise and smoke. Shock will make statues of everyone for a moment, and he will take advantage of it.

And yet he does not come. I think of Honesty as the darkness presses in. What is happening to her? The drip, drip, drip counts out the time. Perhaps he will never come. It is madness to think he could make it out of there. He will be caught and executed. Perhaps he will not give my name and I can live on at the palace, sharing stories with Honesty, warm and safe.

There is the sudden sound of running footsteps and a figure crashes into me. I grab at it, and it struggles to be free.

'It is I, Alice,' I whisper at my brother.

I give him the clothes I am holding for him and help him dress quickly, fixing his wig to his head with a cloth bonnet over it. I hope, for I cannot make him out properly in this blackness, he will look like a maid.

'I missed,' he rasps, distraught.

My heart leaps. His plan for murder has been thwarted.

'We must escape or be killed.' They will know from his clothes that an insider helped and the trail will soon lead to me.

We rush back up from the cellars. There are calls and shouts and people race along the passageways this way and that. My brother stays at my side as I lead the way.

We head past the great kitchens, and the kitchen master's window, out into the gardens. The snow, now coming in fast, makes the torches gutter and the fires in the braziers burn low in the damp. Hoping we are not noticed, we hurry past the ponds and the flowerbeds. We hear the shouting and move on in haste. Not running, for that would make us seem guilty, but pretending we are trying to track down the assailant too.

We come to the wash-house gate. I take the key from inside my bodice. Who would think that someone would escape this way? Here the water is channelled down to the Thames. Here we can wade out through it. Risk drowning if we must – there are far worse ways to die.

'This way.' I signal my brother to follow me. We will flee along the river to the wherry. From there we will go to the Port of London and straight onto a ship bound for France. My brother told me he has secured monies and safe passage.

We go straight into the water, splashing and making too much noise, until we are in up to our shins. I lose the bag of trinkets Honesty had given me somewhere in the water but do not have time to search. The wash channel has been dug close to the palace walls and is shallow, but as we wade along it it deepens and sucks at our clothes, begging to pull us out into the Thames. That will be too powerful for us to survive. It will take us down into its depths. I clutch my brother's hand and he mine, as we gasp in shock at the piercing cold and help each other across the wash channel and out the other side.

Then we run, him behind me swearing, our clothes clinging to our skin, slowing us, dragging us down. At the Thames, I turn to him. In the moonlight, I can make him out as he rips the bonnet and wig from his head and clambers out of his skirt, kicking it violently.

'Where is our boat?' I ask.

'All this and she still lives.' He spits.

'Where is our boat?'

'There is no boat, Alice. You didn't actually think we were going to France, did you? With what? We have nothing. Don't you understand, you stupid girl?'

The breath is taken from me. My insides are hollow, my mouth salty with shock.

'I cannot believe we have actually escaped.' He barks a laugh. 'I thought we would be killed.'

I cannot speak.

'We must part ways now, Alice. I cannot be linked to you, nor you to I.'

Dumbstruck. Empty. Light.

'Alice, you must run. Away from here. As far as you can get. Do not go back. Do you understand?' he hisses.

I cannot feel anything.

'Never speak of me again. And never, ever look for me. Do you understand, Alice?'

'But France…' I barely make a noise.

'I hope you get there,' he says, then suddenly alert, looks behind me.

'Alice?' It is Honesty.

He grabs me and flings me hard towards her, then runs.

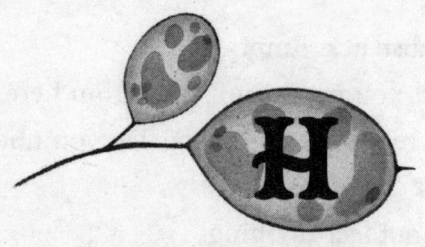

## CHAPTER NINETEEN
# HONESTY

The snow is thick as I follow Alice. It is hard to keep her and her brother in my sight.

Alice and her brother! It was he who pointed the pistol at the Queen. He who tried to murder her. I should go back right now. Let Alice run. If she is caught, she will be killed and in a slow and painful way. If I am caught chasing her, they will think we are in this together. I am not ready to die and yet I cannot stop.

At the channel, I almost give up, but do not. I leap some of the water, but land knee deep and my skirts are soaked. I follow them till they stop on the banks of the Thames. Listen to them argue. Need to speak.

'Alice.'

He flings her at me.

'Go back, Honesty. Quickly.' Terror fills her voice as she hauls herself up from the ground.

'What have you done, Alice?' Even now I am hoping for an explanation. That this has all been a mistake. 'What have you done?' I ask again, though I fear that I already know. 'Why?' This one small word holds so many questions.

'You know as well as I that we do not rule our own lives.'

'But you could have asked me for help. You could have…'

My words run out because I know that they are not true. I have travelled hundreds of miles from my father to have freedom. Alice has not been so lucky. I grasp hold of her. She tries to fight loose, but I hold her firm. I don't want to lose her. My only real friend.

She speaks in haste. 'My father and my brother would have had me killed. What choice did I have?'

'But now you will be murdered anyway.' My words sound so cruel.

'If I am caught.' She struggles to free herself. I

don't let her go. I don't know why. I should let her escape, but my fear won't let me. What will I be here without her?

My thoughts race wildly, searching for a plan. 'You can hide your part in it. We will cover it up. I will lie for you.'

That I would risk so much for her is a surprise even to me, but I know I would. This girl has helped me since I first arrived in London; this girl has made me laugh and shared her tales. 'We can make up a story to cover this. We can, Alice. Let me try.'

There is a pause as she thinks. Snow floats around us like swan feathers and the whole night seems like a dream we can wake from.

'They do not know he is your brother,' I continue. A plan starts to take shape in my mind. 'You can deny all knowledge of him.'

My thoughts gather speed. Perhaps we can get through this. 'We chased him. You and I, together. That's why we are outside the palace gates. We saw him making his escape and we tried to catch him.'

'He is my brother,' she mutters. How her heart must be tearing. I know what it is to be torn to pieces by your family.

'I know, but you must look out for yourself, Alice.' The snow has soaked my clothes and my feet burn from the icy water. I listen for voices coming after us, but hear nothing except the calls from the boats on the river, the far-off promise of the sea.

'It's no use. I stored clothes in the tunnels for him. He left his old clothes there.'

'He could have done that alone.'

'How did you know he was my brother?'

'When I saw the troupe arrive, I recognised him from the tavern and I asked one of the actors, the boy who plays the girl; he told me that your brother had a sister at the palace…'

There is the fault in my plan. I feel it swell in the darkness. The boy knew that the player had a sister at the palace. He will give up this information when he is questioned. Why wouldn't he? If they suspect him of concealing anything, he will be tortured and perhaps rowed through Traitor's Gate.

'We will think of something,' I say, hopelessly.

Alice slaps me hard across the face. The blow winds me. She strikes me again, so hard that my thoughts are knocked from me. I cannot speak as she pulls me close to her.

'You came after me, Honesty.' Her words are

urgent, as she holds me so close to her face I feel her breath hot against my skin. 'You were trying to catch me. I am a traitor. You worked it out. I attacked you.'

'No.' My cheeks are wet. Whether it is tears, blood or snow, I do not know.

'You caught me. We fought. I got away.'

She pushes me from her. I reach out and catch at her dress, but it slips through my fingers, and I fall, the snow thick enough to cushion me. I hear the thud, thud, thud of Alice's feet running, and I am left here, with snow covering me so quickly it will bury me, and the calls from the Thames echoing through the night.

## CHAPTER TWENTY

# ALICE

I return to make sure that Honesty goes back. She lies on the ground. I do not go close, for I don't want her to see me, but I need to know that she is well enough to stand. She is so still I am afraid that I have really hurt her. I didn't want to injure her, but I had no choice. Unless I caused her actual harm, they may think she was a part of the plot.

I step further away as she groans and hauls herself to her knees. I want to go to comfort her, but I must stand firm. There are people out there looking for me. I can hear their shouts now and yet I cannot save myself until I know that she is safe. I wait for her to call the guards. To send them after me. She does not. She just sits there in the snow.

I want to go back and explain to her how my father used to make fine materials for the Queen. How she had dismissed him when the fashions changed and he never recovered. He began gambling and drinking, bringing shame on my mother, and he blames his misfortune for my mother's death. He blames the Queen for all of it. *That's why he is destitute now, Honesty*, I want to say. *That's why he lives on the streets.* He was once a good man, I'm certain he must have been, for my mother was happy and I have some fond memories of my childhood.

My father's need for revenge overcame him. It poisoned him, twisting through his thoughts. I want to tell her how hard it was for him and how hard it still is. To convince her that I had no choice. I didn't want the Queen to be hurt but I was afraid, coward that I am.

I am still afraid.

Honesty crawls forward. She reaches for something. I cannot make out what. She staggers to stand. She inspects the thing she has picked up from the ground. What can it be?

Suddenly, instinctively, I know. It is my mother's pomander, that has hung from my waist since she died. I feel for it, but it is gone. It must have snapped off during our tussle. I am weightless without it. I am spinning, floating like a cloud above myself.

I cannot go back for it.

I must go back for it.

I cannot go back for it.

I watch as Honesty turns to go. Let her have it. It is as much a part of me as my own heart. Perhaps, one day, she will look at it fondly and forgive me.

I wait until she has completely vanished from view and then turn and run. Along the river, towards London.

Now I have nothing. No employment. No money. A ruined reputation. When they find the clothes and piece the events together with my disappearance, they will hunt me down.

There is only one place I can go. It will take hours to walk to Southwark, but I will follow the path of the river and pray my father will help.

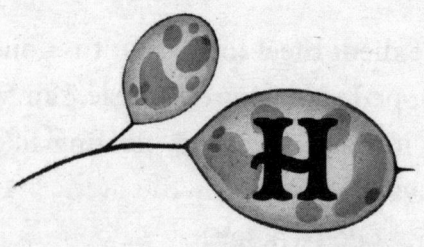

## CHAPTER TWENTY-ONE
# HONESTY

The pomander would bring Alice back if anything would. I hold it close. The snapped cord is sopping but I tie it to the chain at my waist anyway to keep it safe. It makes little difference for I am wet through already.

Maude is at the entrance to the large gardens when I return. It is heavily guarded now. I have not thought beyond my struggle with Alice and my heartache at her leaving and have no idea what I'm going to say.

'What has happened to you?' she asks.

'I fell into a holly bush in the chaos.' My lame excuse is as transparent as a window. The guards move forward, ready to arrest me. I prepare for the worst.

'Yes, I am sorry I sent you beyond the walls to get holly. I needed to bring more into the palace for luck after this terrible event.' Maude pauses for the fraction of a second. 'This way.' She pulls me swiftly with her. The guards say nothing. I think they are afraid of her.

I follow her to the kitchen garden. She has me tight by the arm, and she bids me use snow to clean my face. I do, feeling how swollen my cheek is and gasping at the cold.

Maude whispers harshly, 'Did you play a part in this?'

Trembling, I shake my head. 'On my mother's soul, I am innocent.'

'I believe you. If anyone questions you, you were gathering holly and know nothing else. Tidy your hair and go to your work immediately.'

'Why?' It is not a question about getting to work. I am asking her why she is helping me when it's so dangerous.

'Your story gave my daughter hope.' She smooths her cap into place with her palms. 'She's been searching the gardens for feathers ever since.'

I think back to the girl crying in the garden. The story I told that day, when the Queen first saw me from the window. How much has changed since then. How much I've changed. I start weeping, and Maude puts her arms around me, saying *shush* and patting the back of my head.

'Thank you.' I say.

'We women must help each other.'

With effort, I pull myself together.

Maude goes inside and I take a moment to breathe. The courtyard windows are lit on all four sides. I can hear a harpsichord. Tidying my hair as much as I can and straightening my clothes, I prepare myself for questions. They'll want to know what happened to Alice, once they realise she's missing. I'll have to convince them that I know nothing about her disappearance. She has done me a favour roughing me up a little, I can see that now. I wonder how I will find Alice, to tell her she is the truest friend I have ever had, as I cross the courtyard and head into the chapel passageway.

I hide the pomander beneath my skirt, in case anyone recognises it, and go to the serving hatches near the kitchens. There is much talk of the assassination attempt, naturally, but also, now that the food has all been delivered, there is a mixture of exhaustion and elation at having finished their work.

'What happened to you?' someone I have never seen before asks me as soon as I walk in. Everyone wants to know everyone's business here. I consider weaving an elaborate story, but I am too exhausted.

'Fell into some holly.'

Hoots of laughter. Crackling fire. Leftovers being devoured.

I go to find the ladies-in-waiting to make sure that I am seen. Once the commotion has died down, my absence will raise suspicion.

The Queen has gone to her chambers, though many of the guests are still partying. The ladies-in-waiting have departed. They must have gone to comfort the Queen, or to their own rooms. I search for them. As I approach the courtyard, I hear laughter so loud and happy, it is almost an insult, considering everything I've been through and everything Alice is facing out there in the cruel night.

What will become of her? I picture her frozen body on the cold, hard ground. I think of her hiding in the hollow of a snow-covered tree. I imagine her drowned and rolling out to sea. I want to think she boards a fine galleon and escapes to France to begin a new life.

Laughter teases me back to the present.

I use my elbows to push my way through the throng at the door. Some of the maids remark on my dress, dishevelled as it is now, and my ripening bruises. I push past them and see, to my astonishment, Barnaby standing on one of the tables. Everyone is looking up at him, ladies-in-waiting, nobles and servants, smiling or coaxing him on.

He parades around the tabletop like an actor onstage. He hesitates momentarily when he sees me, then continues to play for his audience. Quietening them by pushing his hands down, he then turns his palms face up to encourage noise from them again. They laugh. I think he is going to sing a madrigal. Or perhaps he has been dancing for them. He is often practising his steps. Much as I would like to join in with the glee, I am weary and must find a space for my bed.

'I give you the tale of the lying girl and how she came to her death.'

He is parodying me and the way I begin my

stories. I am fixed to the spot by this. How dare he?

'Part one. Once there was a maid who believed herself to be better than the rest.'

He gets a raucous response. These people are too drunk to care about whether his story is told with care and craft. They will make do with any entertainment when they are in this slurring state. Once people have decided to have fun, there is no stopping them. An attempt on the Queen's life will not ruin their evening. When the veil is lifted, they seem callous and self-centred. All shouting and cajoling and pushing for attention. Where are my friends now that they have a new storyteller? Who cares about me when I have given them everything I've got?

Barnaby prances about the makeshift stage, keeping his audience waiting.

'This girl told lies. Said that she was quick and clever. She was nothing but a fool.'

He hops about here, as a jester would, in a silly manner, and they cry out in delight, rapping the table for more.

'The fool...' He repeats the dance to even more rowdiness, then laughing himself, lights a pipe and smokes as he waits for hush. 'The fool thought herself very fine. "I'm a lady," she said to anyone who would hear her. "Look at my curtsey."' Prancing about the tabletop, he curtsies badly, pretending to wobble. '"I will go to the ball," the fool told everyone.'

I feel my skin prickle and my throat tighten. Barnaby seeks me out, his eyes glinting.

'The fool's head swelled to the size of a globe, convinced how important she was.' He pretends to be downcast as if he cannot believe how sad this is. 'Little did the fool know that she was an idiot.'

They clap each other's hands and guzzle drinks.

'Or that she was swelling like a pig's bladder with her high thoughts of herself.'

Roars of laughter. I am shoved back and stand in the doorway, watching, leaning against the wall to keep me up.

'The night of the ball arrived, and the *idiot* called for her gown.'

They shriek at the repeat of the word idiot. If only I had known it was so easy to entertain them, I think bitterly.

'She tried to put it on but found it did not fit. For her body had swelled so much with her arrogance, and her idiocy, and her stupidness, it was too tight.' Acting as if he is sorry for her, he walks the table, the audience in the palm of his hand.

'She went to the ball in her tight dress, convinced she looked like a lady. But as the music played and the guests entered, her self-importance swelled so much, her dress began to split. Pop, pop, pop.' He pretends to be bursting out of his clothes. 'It split and ripped and tore and the holes left her flapping in the wind.'

One of the ladies laughs so much, she pukes into her goblet.

'In desperation, she stole a brooch.'

I feel my legs give way. Holding to the wall, I stare at him. The treacherous enemy.

'But the brooch was not enough to fix her dress, and she deserved it to be ruined, for she was a spiteful soul, with no friends.'

He waits a moment, then turns in my direction, though no one else would know he was speaking to me.

'She was arrested for the brooch she stole and her big, globe-sized head was chopped off and rolled into the Thames.'

He bows to hurrahs.

I see it. He was there, in the ladies' dressing room for a moment before the brooch disappeared. It was he who ruined my dress too. He is always around. He wanted his revenge for the time I used him in my tale.

And Alice. I blamed her for all that happened. Oh, what a woeful girl I am.

Perhaps Barnaby's tale is no less than I deserve. My cheeks flaming, I leave him to his audience, and walk the passages in thought.

There was no way I could defend myself against Barnaby's story. And he knew it. I must stay meek now. Laugh along with others to gain popularity, to avert suspicion. I can pretend to have many friends amongst the maids, can't I? I smile at a few and wave as I pass. Some return my smile, others look away. No one is what they seem here. We will all be questioned, and I am glad of my bruises to defend me. Perhaps they will make the difference. They and Maude's assistance might just save my skin.

Whatever happens now, the court will never be the same for me and I will never trust anyone again.

## CHAPTER TWENTY-TWO

# ALICE

It is morning when I reach Southwark. This place I know too well. This is the corner where I ran screeching from my brother as we played tag, waiting for my father to leave the tavern. This ground where I marked out hopscotch with a stick and hopped between squares while he was betting on dogs, or bears. This is where I stared at the ever-changing glimpses of sky between close-knit roofs when my brother began to follow my father's ways. Southwark has not changed much, but I am a different person, and this feels part of a very different life.

I keep my hood low so that no one can see my face. I do not want to be here, but what choice do I have?

How lucky those at the palace are. Even those with the hardest jobs have a place to sleep without fear of freezing to death.

My father haunts these streets, begging help from former friends and stealing where he must. He has survived this long. He must help me. Or at least hide me for a few days while I plan my escape to another country. I see people's eyes fix on me as my hood is pulled back by the wind, then slide away. Word will soon reach him that I'm here. Some of these people have known me for years and they do not forget a face.

I pass the tanners, the sound of knives scraping hides familiar as a heartbeat, and the pie shop, drooling at the pies on display. If only I had not believed my brother and had hidden some savings for myself. I speed up to stay warm, always on my toes in case someone tries to capture me.

There is a tug at my skirts, and I whip round to defend myself. Looking down, I see a boy of some six years or so. He is holding up a pie. Eel pie, I think, from the delicious aroma wafting from the holes in its thick-crust pastry.

'My pa wants to give you this.'

In fear of a trap or poison, I resist it, starved as I am.

'Why? Who is your pa?'

The boy points back at the pie shop.

'He says it's for you, Alice. He saw you passing. He says you are welcome to it.'

I take it and devour it, letting it burn my gullet and warm my insides.

The boy stands, rolling some marbles in his small palms. 'He says that everyone's been told to watch for you and that you should get out of here and don't come back.'

Bad news is passed on quicker than the plague in Southwark. A reward for a traitor even quicker than that. The boy runs off, and as I watch him go, I see my father. He is crouching outside a tavern, which is no surprise. He beckons to me, which is.

When I get close enough, he grabs my arm and drags me into an alley, so thin it is hardly more than a crease between houses. Shaking myself free, I lean far enough away from him that he cannot quite reach me, and his fists fall short of their target.

'What are you doing here?' His eyeballs roam wildly, as if he is being chased or is drunk – or both. Spittle lands on his chin. 'Have you been followed?

Do you want your father to be murdered? Are you mad?'

'Perhaps I am.' I once felt sorrow for him. Seeing him again, I now feel only disgust. 'What am I to do, Father? You must help me.'

'I've helped you enough.' He glares at me with hatred, but I am strong against him and glare back. I am his property. I must force him to help me.

'I did what you asked of me and now I have nothing. No way to make a living for myself.'

Someone walks past us, and he pulls me closer so that he can hide behind me. This tells me there is no hope. Whoever my father was when my mother was alive, that man has gone.

'Where is my brother?' I ask in desperation.

'He's dead. As good as. Caught and to be executed.'

I sway and he grips hold of my arm. Memories of my brother flash before me. Now he will never grow old.

'That girl. Sybil, her name is. She told them all her part in it and all yours too.'

Sybil! It was she who grabbed me from behind and gave me my orders. To think that once I imagined we could be friends!

They will come for me too now they know.

'Please.' I beg of my father, for what else can I do? 'Please.'

Perhaps, if I were a man, I would be able to make a new life for myself, but as a girl…

'You are my father.' It's an accusation and he flinches.

'I'm sorry.' And he is gone. Creeping out of my life forever.

'I am sorry too.' I whisper.

He told himself a story that revenge would solve everything. It seems so pointless now. I know he will learn nothing. I know he will come up with another version of the story, someone else to blame for all that has happened to him. Perhaps he will blame me.

Not knowing what else to do, I hide here in this corner until the light disappears and I am part of the night.

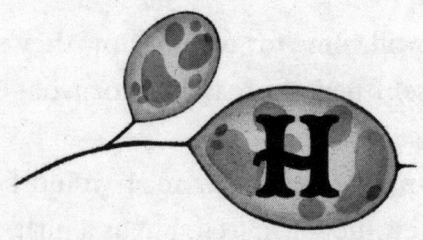

## CHAPTER TWENTY-THREE
# HONESTY

We are moving to Richmond Palace. Treachery has stained the festivities here and nobody feels safe. It's not a moment too soon, for the stench from the latrines is ripe enough to curdle milk. The air steams yellow and rumours of plague are rife.

The Queen has gone ahead, with everyone important. I have had to make this one last errand to fetch material for their new clothes. Now I am nothing but a maid who carts and fetches and scrubs and washes. Gone are my chances at parties and feasts. Gone is my beautiful gown.

I start to feel sorry for myself, but then I remember everything that was awful about being in the eye of the Queen and the ladies-in-waiting.

I see it now in Barnaby, struggling for new stories to outdo the last, his look of terror as he sees his popularity ebbing away. A new storyteller will always be waiting for their chance. He has tasted fame for a short while, but you must maintain your place. If you are not born to it, you have to prove that you deserve it again and again, until you cannot sleep, eat, think. All you can do is worry what people say of you. How you must make them like you when you no longer like yourself.

I will share some of my stories with him if he asks, but I will not volunteer them. I am surprised by how often I have to resist the urge to help him. I picture Alice sewing through the night to mend the dress he slashed and that stalls my generous spirit.

In the city, I see her in everyone who passes.

Here, a hooded figure dashing past. There, in a milliner's trying on a hat. A face racing by in a carriage. Before me, behind me, disappearing around a corner. And yet, none of them are her. With heavy heart, I go about my business.

Before I leave London, I want to hear a play. I am due at Richmond, but I am so close to the Globe that I cannot resist listening outside for a moment.

The flags snap in the wind against a bruised

sky. The play has begun. I stand outside. The wind, mean and greedy, snatches some words away, but I catch small parts. A smile plays on my lips as I think of the way that the play casts its spell over the noisiest watcher. The way the story makes spines straighten to see, wives scold their husbands into quiet, people shout in alarm when there is danger coming. My mother taught me stories so I would always be free and yet since Alice left my words seem drained of colour.

Breaking away from the theatre, I know I have all those stories inside me, close to my skin. I hope that one day I will be happy enough to speak them again.

A flash of yellow catches at the corner of my eye. I look across, expecting nothing.

Can it be? No, I cannot believe it. And yet...

She is crouched down, hunched. Our eyes meet. I walk to her and she stands, using the wall behind her as support. An invisible string pulls us together.

'Alice.'

'Honesty.'

We are suspended in time, in a bubble of joy at simply seeing one another again.

The wind switches direction, bringing me back

to my senses. The world comes alive. People bustle about, shouting wares. The noise from the theatre carries to us. A flock of bothered geese honk past. I see, in horror, that Alice looks starved. Her hair hangs lank, and dirt encrusts her clothes. Her nails are broken and her face is blotched purple with cold.

'Alice.' It is my only word. She is alive! But what has happened to her?

She turns to leave. I follow. She does not rush. As we get to the back of the theatre, I put my hand on her shoulder. She stops as if she wanted me to catch her all along.

'I thought you wouldn't want to talk to me again.' She searches my face.

I don't know how to tell her how much I have missed her.

Just then, the play ends and crowds start to pour out. Taking Alice by the hand, I pull her into the shadows. By some miracle, we find a corner of the world to hide in alone.

'Here.' I have some dried figs which I have brought with me to eat. She takes a couple and swallows them almost whole.

'I have been looking for you, Alice. I am about to move to Richmond. It was my last chance to find you.'

She nods. Were things the other way around, she would have looked for me too.

'I wanted to tell you how truly sorry I am.' My skin prickles with guilt. 'It was Barnaby who took the brooch and shredded my gown.'

She gives another nod. 'I have had a lot of time to think since I left the palace and I suspected as much.'

'I needed to apologise and to give you this.'

I press the pomander into her palm. She cups it between both hands as if it were a precious bird. Her face shines with relief. It is the greatest treasure either of us has held in a long time.

'Thank you, Honesty.' She keeps her gaze on the pomander. 'I behaved so horribly to you.'

'No. It was I who…'

'Let me speak. I must say it. I was so afraid. Every moment I was at the palace, I had to go unnoticed so that, my brother, my father…' She searches my face for understanding and finds it. 'And then you came along with your courage and stories, so bright and vibrant and bold.'

I try to speak again but she is firm.

'How I envied you.' One tear, plump and clear, rolls over her cheekbone, leaving a line in the dirt.

'And how I liked you. And I *could* not be friends. I *should not* have been friends.'

She will not give way to me easily, but I insist. 'And how I envied you, Alice. Your thoughtfulness, gentle and delicate. Your quietness is a part of you. They took advantage of it, yes, but it is your way, Alice. And with that comes reasoning and regard. A person who notices the small things that other people cast aside. When you speak, it is because you have something to say, not for attention or simply to make a noise, but because your words are from somewhere deep within you. It is I who should be sorry. Marching into your life, shouting about what I thought was important then and know to be nothing now.'

We hug each other in earnest and when we break, I wrinkle my nose to make light of the rank smell of her clothes and she thumps my shoulder in jest.

'Alice,' I confess.

'Yes?'

'I freed Puck.'

I tell her how I sneaked into the ladies-in-waiting's chamber when they were dining in the Great Hall. How I unfastened the squirrel's cage and took him out, giving him walnuts to keep him from biting me, hiding him under my cloak. How I smuggled him from the palace.

'I took the chain from his neck and pointed to the woods beyond the gardens. He didn't trust me at first, but then he hopped off and climbed a tree. He sat staring at me from the lowest bough. I threw hazelnuts to him, then filled a hole in the tree with them where he could see me, so he is well-stocked for the winter, and buried a pile shallowly elsewhere while he watched.'

'Will Bridgette know that it was you who set him free?'

'I left his cage open and the window unlatched and wide. She thought she had forgotten to bolt the lock and that he had opened the window himself.' I pull an expression of absolute disbelief at Bridgette's naivety and see it mirrored by a smiling Alice.

'She always did like a good story.'

The theatre crowd has dispersed now, besides a few stragglers. Time is passing. Richmond Palace waits.

'Will he go back to his gilded cage, do you think?' Alice asks. 'Or will he take his freedom?'

'I don't know, but at least the choice is in his own hands.'

'It isn't. The choice is in his paws.'

And together we laugh and eat figs.

## CHAPTER TWENTY-FOUR
# ALICE

'Look.' Honesty gestures to some of the players coming out of the theatre. With much shouting and quarrelling, they are loading up a cart. 'They must be going on the road.'

'Yes. Were they questioned, Honesty? Because of what I did?'

'Because of what your father and your brother did.' Honesty shuffles from foot to foot. 'They were not.'

I know it is a lie and some of their company is missing. 'I think they are wise to take to the road for a while.'

We watch as they carry out trunks and baskets, then cover them against the snow with thick sacking. They tie it all down with rope, but it is too slack for this savage wind and the covering billows like a sail.

'It is like the cabbage cart I arrived on. I was a different person then, Alice.'

The light is bleeding from the sky and the wet ground soaks through my shoes. My lips are cracked and my sore throat makes my words croaky and painful. 'Oh, to be free to go on the road. Discover adventures and be as brave as you were.'

Honesty turns to me. 'I have material for clothes.' She points to her package.

'Yes, you must get it to Richmond.'

'I became a new person once already. I can do it again.'

'I do not know what you mean, Honesty.'

A shiver convulses my body and I do not know that I will survive another night in this ravaging cold.

'We have means.' Honesty shows me some coins she has in her purse. 'We have clothes. We have a method of escape. Come with me on an adventure.'

She points to the cart, and I see her plan.

'It is too dangerous. You must go back. You have prospects and a great future with the Queen. You must go to Richmond now and forget about me.'

'I will not.' She stands firm, her hands on her hips. Aye, she is headstrong. 'We were meant to meet, Alice. Fortune has brought me to you. First, here in London. Then at the palace. And now, to find you again. We were meant to help each other. Fate wants us to be friends. It is written in the stars. See?'

She points upwards and I nod. The sky is bright with snowflakes, which look like falling stars. 'I see.'

The men have gone back inside.

'They will be in danger if they are caught with me, Honesty.'

'No one will recognise you when we are away from here. We are just two runaways, hitching a lift.' The horse hoofs the floor and snorts white streaming jets of steam. 'There, behold, our dragon.' Honesty uses the voice she does when telling stories to an audience.

A flicker of something stirs in me. I want to live and hope again. There is this life here, cold and hungry, with fear in every step. There is another life somewhere else, if we go together.

'Our dragon grows impatient.' The horse whinnies and stamps with perfect timing. We burst out laughing then stop at once, looking at each other, realising how serious this is.

Honesty. Bold. Brash. Brave. Can I be that too?

I take a step out of the shadows. The light catches the Thames and makes it beautiful, like a necklace of diamonds or an exquisite silver chain. No, it is more beautiful because it is real and there for everyone. Can I leave this place?

At first, we sneak, then stride with purpose. To pass unnoticed you must look as if you know where you are going. We need to move now or miss our chance.

Honesty has to push me up into the cart for I am in pain to my very bones. Once in, I put my hands out to yank her up too. Snow begins to tumble as we pull the sacking over us. We huddle down amidst the costumes and wait to be found and thrown out. Holding each other close, we hear the players return. We barely breathe. Arguing how one of them should learn to pause before entering, they do not take time to check the back of the cart and tighten the ropes above us. Others call that they will follow on and we wait for what seems an eternity for them to climb into the driver's seat. As the cart judders to a start, I clutch Honesty's hand in excitement. We are moving.

Taking the chance to peek out, I say a proper farewell to Southwark, the place which has brought me into the world and taken so much from me. I want to remember the happy times I had here.

'Goodbye.' I whisper, watching as we trundle away until the Thames is out of sight.

'A new adventure,' Honesty whispers to me.

'A new life.'

Some friends become a part of our own story. Without them, we cannot become who we are destined to be. Here, as this cart jolts, taking us off into the snow-spun night, we do not know what will happen to us, or where we will end up, but we are starting our own tale this time and for that we are both ready.

# ACKNOWLEDGEMENTS

At the beginning of this story, Honesty very bravely walks into the unknown alone. I'm not as brave as her so I'm very grateful to have had a band of merry wanderers at my side as this book was created. I owe thanks to so many people.

Thanks first to readers. This story wouldn't exist without you. You are my people.

To my editor and friend, Janet Thomas. What a joy it has been to create these stories with you. We have a saying in our house when something preposterous or improbable happens – 'It wouldn't get past Janet'. I will miss the magic you bring.

Huge thanks to my agent, Kate Shaw. I never feel alone in this world of writing as part of Team Shaw. Thank you for your support, wit, expertise and friendship. I am the luckiest writer to have you on my side.

Cynthia Paul and Becka Moor for the stunning cover illustration and design. Karen Bultiauw,

Rebecca Lloyd, Amy Low and all the team at Firefly Press for your hard work, dedication and dragon-hearted braveness.

My beautiful mum who is basically an unpaid researcher for me, and my gorgeous dad who loves to chat about how many words we've both written daily. I wouldn't be a writer without you. To Jo, Ro, Razmo and Alfredo, for all the little things but especially the treacle tart.

To my friends Ness Harbour, Jane Fraser, Matt Brown, Jane 'Bobby' Charlton, for saying beautiful and funny things. And to all the Hay Festival – Writers at Work, for their wisdom, camaraderie and generosity.

Tiffany Murray, Michael Read, Stevie Davies. Without the belief of such wonderful people, I would never have been able to believe in myself. I can't thank you enough.

The young writers and readers at Tonyrefail Community School for their inspiration, enthusiasm and general brilliance. A huge thanks to Cara

Marvelley, who is one of the best people I've ever met.

Melanie Knapp at the Tudor Merchant's House, Tenby, and all the staff at Hampton Court Palace and the Globe Theatre, who answered a thousand questions.

This book couldn't have been written without the support of Books Council Wales, the Society of Authors and Literature Wales. Thank you to them for all the work they do to support authors.

Lastly, and most importantly, to my husband, Guy, and my dog, Watson Jones. You have made my life. Diolch.